THE SPIRIT FLYER SERIES

BICYCLE HILLS

How One Halloween Almost Got Out of Hand

JOHN BIBEE

Illustrated by Paul Turnbaugh

INTERVARSITY PRESS
DOWNERS GROVE, ILLINOIS 60515

InterVarsity Press is the book-publishing division of InterVarsity Christian Fellowship, a student movement active on campus at hundreds of universities, colleges and schools of nursing. For information about local and regional activities, write Public Relations Dept., InterVarsity Christian Fellowship, 6400 Schroeder Rd., P.O. Box 7895, Madison, WI 53707-7895.

Cover illustration: Paul Turnbaugh

ISBN 0-8308-1203-2

Printed in the United States of America

Library of Congress Cataloging-in-Publication Data

Bibee, John.
  Bicycle hills.

  (The Spirit Flyer series; 4)
  Summary: Secret bicycle games in a new amusement park lead the young cyclists into an adventure of magic and a battle against evil.

  [1. Fantasy] I. Turnbaugh, Paul, ill. II. Series: Bibee, John. Spirit Flyer series; 4.
PZ7.B47146Bi 1989   [Fic]   89-15316
ISBN 0-8308-1203-2

13   12   11   10   9   8   7   6   5
99   98   97   96   95

For Will and Maria

NEW
IN
TOWN
· · · · · · · ·

1

Once there was a town full of children who wanted to dream their lives away. Times were hard. So they tried to run away to the secret place of their dreams. No one knew that the borders of this place crossed over into the Deeper World. But no one worried because this place was more fun than they had ever dreamed. . . .

A lot of changes had come to the small town of Centerville by fall. School had started in September, but that was about the only thing that seemed normal anymore. Since the summer, life had gotten hard there like everywhere else in the world. At first it had been called a recession, and then it was called the Great Depression of the Nineties. Banks had closed, businesses had failed, and even the government was on the verge of bankruptcy. Inflation had kept rising. In some places there were shortages of food and gasoline. A record number of people had lost their jobs. Many had lost everything they owned in a few months.

Centerville, like the rest of the world, was covered by a shadow of fear: fear that there wouldn't be enough food to eat, fear of sickness and no money to get help, fear that tomorrow would bring war and things even worse, things so terrible that no one wanted to think about them. For many people, life seemed to be falling apart in a chain reaction, and no one seemed to know how to make it stop.

The little town of Centerville, like most places, was trying to find its way back to the peace and prosperity it used to enjoy before the depression. And ever since Goliath Industries had reopened the old factory on the outside of town, things had been changing. Most people liked the changes brought on by Goliath Industries. By the beginning of October, many of the townspeople were working at the factory with good, well-paying jobs. Since times were uncertain, having money in the bank and food on the table had become more important than ever.

Goliath Industries brought many new people to Centerville as new jobs opened up at the factory. The Burke family moved to Centerville because of the new jobs. Dr. Burke, a scientist, had worked for Goliath for over a year and had been transferred to work on research and development at the reopened factory. Dr. Burke and his wife had an eleven-year-old daughter named Amy, and a new baby named Sarah Jane. The baby, of course, was too young to know that she had even moved to a new town. But Amy, who was in the sixth grade, wasn't having as easy a time in making the change.

Even before the move, Amy felt as if her world had been changed too much over the past year. She had felt unhappy much of the time, and moving to Centerville had only made things worse. Deep inside, Amy felt as if something was wrong, as if something was broken. But how could a person be broken, she wondered to herself?

Amy had short, curly brown hair and hazel eyes. She was average height for her age and quite strong. She had lived in Centerville for two weeks before she felt somewhat settled. But just knowing the names of the streets and stores and the address of your house doesn't make a person feel at home in a new place. Something was still missing in her life.

"It's Friday afternoon and I should feel better than this," she said wearily to herself as she rode her bike away from the school parking lot. She was glad to be out of school, and the cool October air felt fresh on her face. She pedaled her blue ten-speed bicycle slowly, lost inside her thoughts.

She had only ridden two blocks before the bad feelings seemed so strong she felt as if she could touch them. They hung on her like a heavy overcoat. The feelings were hard to describe, but it was something like being lost and scared. When she was a young girl she had once gotten lost in a department store and couldn't find her father and stepmother. At first she had felt scared, then the fear grew into panic the more she looked for her parents and couldn't find them. When she finally saw them by a checkout counter, she had burst into tears. She had felt foolish for being so scared because they hadn't even realized she was gone. But then she was troubled because she wondered why they hadn't noticed she was missing.

"But I'm not lost now," Amy told herself, feeling foolish for even thinking such a thing. Being lost was almost impossible in a town as small as Centerville, even if she had only lived there two weeks. Still, she had to admit that she felt lost, and she wasn't sure why.

Amy turned a corner and pedaled up a street without bothering to look at the street sign. She was pedaling her bike, but she didn't really have a destination. She knew she didn't really want to go home to her new house. But she didn't know where she wanted to go.

Being out of school for the day meant freedom, but free to do what?

The whole weekend was ahead of her. All day during school Amy had dreamed of the moment when she would be outside, free to do what she wanted. But now that school was over and her dream had arrived, it wasn't like she had imagined it. Her freedom was quickly turning into restless boredom. Having no place to go was not the same as being lost, but it was almost as bad, she thought to herself.

"If I wasn't stuck in this stupid little town I could be having fun," Amy said. She squeezed the brake and stopped, waiting. For a moment she wished she lived in her old house in the suburbs. She sighed, then turned her bicycle around and pedaled toward her new home.

Amy's family lived in the newest, most expensive section of Centerville called Buckingham Estates. Their new house was nice enough, but it still didn't seem very homey to the girl, not like their old house. That house had been big with creaky wooden floors and wooden steps and a large comfortable attic filled with all sorts of delightful junk. Amy's father said the old house had a personality, but Amy's stepmother wanted a new modern house which was easy to keep clean and didn't have to be repaired every other weekend.

Amy pedaled up the driveway and parked. She frowned at the lawn. It had rained the night before and the yard looked pathetic. Pieces of sod were lined up in rows like little square grassy islands on top of a sea of mud. The grass hadn't really rooted and her stepmother had instructed Amy not to play on it. The grass was already turning brown and dingy from the cool weather. Amy didn't see how you could even call it a real yard yet. She parked her bike, got her books and went inside the house. The baby was crying.

Having a baby in the house was something Amy still wasn't used to. She had been an only child for years. Her real mother had died when Amy was three. Her father married again when Amy was six. One month before moving to Centerville, little Sarah Jane Burke was born. Amy's stepmother was named Jane. Amy thought the baby was kind of cute, but she didn't think little Sarah Jane would ever be like a real sister since she was so much younger and had a different mother. She was a half sister, her father told her, but Amy wasn't sure she liked having only half of a sister.

"Your teacher called," her stepmother said as Amy walked into the family room. Mrs. Burke was holding little Sarah, patting her on the back. "She said you got another D on a test. That's not like you."

"It was a quiz, not a test," Amy said quickly. By the look on her stepmother's face, Amy could see it didn't make much difference. To her, a D was a D and that was a failing grade.

Because of a bad case of the flu and the move, Amy had missed the start of her sixth grade class. She had lagged behind since she got to Centerville. She felt like she was trying to march in a parade that had started without her. Being in a new school was a big change, but starting out so far behind just made it worse. Though the other children in Amy's class weren't exactly unfriendly, they weren't real easy to get to know either. More than once they had teased her and treated her as if she was stupid because she missed the answers when Mrs. Johnson asked a question.

That frustrated Amy because she knew she wasn't stupid. But she feared she would be labeled a dummy by the rest of the kids. In truth, Amy was a smart and capable child. She was especially good at mathematics and always got A's. But it was also true that she was a somewhat lazy student. She didn't like to study and she had a stubborn streak. If someone told her to study, she just naturally resisted. In the past, she always managed to get good grades in her schoolwork with very little effort, so she did the minimum amount of work to get by. She didn't see why she should work harder than necessary, especially on things she found boring and unchallenging. Since she usually made A's and B's on her report card, she figured that was enough, even if she wasn't doing her best work.

But that day she had made her third D in a row in her geography class quiz. She had been shocked when Mrs. Johnson dropped the paper on her desk. Amy had quickly folded it up and stuffed it in her back pocket. Mrs. Johnson had also talked to Amy after lunch.

"I know it's hard getting adjusted to a new school, especially when you have to catch up to the rest of the class," Mrs. Johnson had said. "I know you're capable, but you can't expect the rest of us to spin our wheels, waiting for you. You'll just have to study harder, Amy." Amy had just nodded silently. She had hoped Mrs. Johnson would be more understanding. As Amy had left the room she wasn't sure if she wanted to cry or just get mad.

"Who cares what the principal exports of Bolivia and Brazil are, anyway?" Amy blurted out to her stepmother.

"Your father and I care that you don't seem to be living up to your potential," Mrs. Burke said. "You don't want a bad report card or a bad score in the Point System. Have you checked your number card lately? I want you to go upstairs and study until supper's ready."

Amy was about to argue when the baby started to wail. She had quickly learned it was impossible to talk to her stepmother when the baby needed attention.

Amy clomped up the stairs to her room. She closed the door, put her books on her desk and flopped down on her bed. She pulled her number card out of her back pocket. A white 78 was on one side of the number card. Amy smiled as she looked at the number. The number card was about the size of a credit card and appeared to be made of black plastic. On the other side of the card was a dark shadowy picture of Amy's face.

"At least my Point System score is good," Amy said to herself and sighed. "I checked my score at the Big Board yesterday. I don't see why Dad and Jane should be upset as long as I'm doing ok in the Point System. The Big Boards know what really counts. Who cares about geography?"

Amy had seen her first Big Board over a year before in her old school. That's when she got her own number card. They also had a huge Big

Board in the factory where her father had worked. Goliath Industries were the inventors of Big Boards and had sold hundreds of thousands of the mysterious panels all over the world. They had sprung up like weeds almost everywhere. You could find them in stores, in banks, in schools and in businesses. The first Big Board in Centerville had been put up in the toy store in August of that year. Amy was surprised that it had taken that long. She figured Centerville was slow in progress because it was just a small town. Since then, a Big Board had been added at the Goliath factory and another one had been put up at the Goliath Bank of Centerville.

Amy had never been quite sure how the mysterious Big Boards worked. They were something like a computerized adding machine and scoreboard. Big Boards were made of a black shiny, plasticlike material in the shape of a rectangle. The smaller ones were usually about seven or eight feet tall, about twenty feet wide and three inches thick. But they could get much bigger than that.

The Point System was the reason Big Boards existed. Everything about a person or group was broken down into points. The Big Boards kept track of these points for the Point System. Amy hadn't liked the Point System because it seemed like another kind of report card, only bigger. The Big Board not only kept track of all the students' grades and scores on tests, but it kept track of almost everything you could imagine—from I.Q. points to grade points to good and bad points to overall personality and popularity points. Then those points, negative and positive, were all added up to form a person's overall point total or score. The higher your overall point total, the better your rank. And the better your rank, the more everyone thought of you.

Amy had resented being ranked in the Point System at first. But like everyone else, she got used to the idea after a while. The Point System had become another unpleasant fact of life. It wasn't really that new of an idea, since the school already ranked children in the overall class standings and so on. And everyone knew who was most popular and who was prettiest and who could run the fastest. The Big Board just made it all Official and kept track of those kinds of things.

A lot of people, especially the more successful children and adults, loved knowing where they ranked among their friends and why. Being a fairly good student from a wealthy family had given Amy a good rank in the Point System in her old school. She was always in the top hundred on the Big Board, and that worked in her favor. Since she was a new-comer to Centerville, she wasn't sure her good standing would transfer. But within a week her rank got better and better until she had ranked in at a respectable seventy-eight. She had assumed her rank would just keep getting better.

Seeing her rank made her feel better. She put the black card in her pocket, then stared out the window toward the back yard. In the dis-tance she could see the tall smokestacks of the Goliath factory. Tarry black smoke drifted steadily into the sky. She wished her father were home. With his new job, he often worked late and missed supper. Amy hated not knowing when he was coming home.

As a scientist, her father was an intense man and broadly educated. He had graduate degrees in both chemistry and physics. Amy had a lot of respect for her father and tried to please him. If it hadn't been for his expectations, she probably wouldn't have gotten as good grades as she did. After her mother had died, her father had spent a lot of time with Amy, and they had grown very close during those three years. Then Jane had come into both of their lives. Her father seemed happier, but Amy missed being the center of his attention.

As she had grown up, she sometimes wondered if her father had really wanted a son. She and her father seemed to have many common interests. Even after Jane came to live with them, Amy had considered herself more like her father. He used to read to her every night. And with his help, she had even learned to read by herself when she was four. He took her to museums and parks, and taught her to use two kinds of computers. He also taught her how to use hand tools, like a hammer and saw and screwdriver. She had always assumed she inherited her ability in math from him.

The thing she had loved to do best, however, was go on nature walks with him. Before they had moved to Centerville, they used to go for walks in a place called Brigadoon Farm. Amy had some of the best times of her life out walking and exploring with her father. Brigadoon Farm had seemed like a piece of paradise on earth to the girl. Even without her father around, Brigadoon Farm was a place full of adventure and fun. Old man Brigadoon, the owner of the farm, had even let Amy ride his old white horse. Amy had loved the horse and called him Pegasus. The horse had been old and barely ever moved faster than a slow walk. Yet Amy had pretended that Pegasus had beautiful white wings, just like the horse in the Greek myth.

But all that was in the past. Amy was in Centerville. Her father was gone much of the time. When their family was transferred to Centerville, she hoped that her father wouldn't be so busy with his work. But after the first week, he seemed busier than ever. Goliath Industries was making everyone work hard on some big secret project, he told Amy. But when she asked what the work was about, he avoided giving direct answers to her questions.

Amy plopped down at her desk and opened her book on geography. She read one sentence. Then she closed the book and turned on the small color television on top of the bookcase. She had watched four reruns when her stepmother called her for supper. Amy flipped off the TV and ran downstairs to the dining room.

Amy frowned when she saw only two plates on the table. Mrs. Burke brought in a casserole and salad bowl.

"Dad isn't coming for supper?" Amy asked. Mrs. Burke nodded. "But that's the third time this week. And it's Friday."

"I don't like it any more than you," her stepmother said.

Amy picked at her food. Supper hardly felt like supper if her dad wasn't there. And halfway through the meal, the baby began crying in the other room. Amy was left eating all alone. She took two more bites of the gooey casserole and then stood up.

"May I go ride my bike?" Amy asked as her stepmother came in the room, bouncing little Sarah Jane up and down. Mrs. Burke nodded, but didn't look at Amy.

Once outside, Amy looked at the sky and figured there was about a half-hour of daylight left. She was trying to decide where she might ride when she heard voices coming from the yard next door. A tall cedar fence separated the two yards. The fence had been put up recently and the cedar boards still had a fresh, spicy smell. Being both bored and curious, Amy walked slowly toward the cedar fence to listen.

She immediately recognized at least two of the voices. They were her neighbors, Tiffany and Sloan Favor. Tiffany was in Amy's sixth-grade class at school and Sloan was a year older. The Favor family had moved to Centerville a few weeks before Amy's family. Mr. Favor was the executive vice president at the Goliath factory, second in importance only to the executive president, an old man named Mr. Cyrus Cutright.

"He only loaned me this stupid bike for an hour," Tiffany said. "He'll get suspicious if I don't bring it back soon. But I do have his permission. I made sure of that. I even got him to put his thumbprint of blood on the form Uncle Bunkie gave me down at the toy store. As long as I have his permission, I can ride it, he said."

"I've got the gas can and matches," Sloan replied. "Everything is ready, but we better hurry. I'll go by David's house and pick him up first. And the rest of you go get Mary Ann. We'll meet you out by the cemetery in fifteen minutes."

Amy paused to listen. She heard the children moving beyond the fence as they got on their bicycles. Amy naturally wondered why her neighbors were going out by the cemetery with a gas can and matches and a borrowed bicycle. Though her first thought was to join them, she figured that this was a secret trip and that she probably wouldn't be welcome. Even though they were neighbors, Amy still didn't know

much about Tiffany and Sloan, except that they were popular and their parents were rich.

"I think I'll just invite myself to this strange little meeting," Amy said to herself. She ran back to her bike and hopped on. She coasted to the street and watched the other children riding away. There seemed to be at least ten children on bikes. Sloan was holding a small rectangular gas can with one hand. Amy waited, not wanting to follow too closely. When the children turned the corner, Amy took off after them.

THE BURNING BIKE

2

The other children seemed to be in a great hurry as they rode down the street, which only made Amy more curious. She hadn't been in Centerville very long, but she did know how to get to the Centerville Cemetery. It was on the same road as the Goliath factory, just beyond the northwest side of town. Since Amy's house was in the southwest part of town, all she had to do was ride north. Then she had a plan. She figured if she pedaled hard, she could reach the cemetery ahead of them. Then she could hide and see what they were up to.

Her neighbors, Tiffany and Sloan, had moved from the city. The Favor family was rich and sophisticated. Sloan was a handsome lanky boy with stylish blond hair, blue eyes and perfect teeth. Tiffany, also blonde, was very pretty, wore the best clothes and had a perfect smile just like Sloan. They looked happy and secure, like children in clothing catalogs. In just a few weeks they had quickly become two of the most popular children in town. Amy admired Tiffany since she was so popular. Tiffany acted as if she could tolerate Amy, but made it clear that they would not be close friends. Tiffany was also a girl that seemed full of secrets. Amy felt like an outsider when she was around Tiffany and her group of friends.

Amy and Tiffany had gotten off to a bad start from the beginning. On Amy's first day at school, Mrs. Johnson had asked Tiffany to do a rather difficult math problem on the blackboard, but the popular girl missed the answer. Without raising her hand, Amy had blurted out that she could do the problem. Mrs. Johnson let Amy try. Amy got the right answer quickly and smiled as Mrs. Johnson praised her. But Tiffany and her group of friends later accused Amy of trying to be the teacher's pet. They had called her "Brainy" and other names. Amy quickly realized she had made a mistake in being so eager to solve the problem. She had tried to pretend it didn't hurt her feelings, but she wished the other girls would include her in their group since they were the most popular kids in the class. Since that first day, Amy had tried not to make Tiffany or the other girls mad, even though they often called Amy names.

Amy knew she had to be careful if she wanted to see what her neighbors were planning. When she saw that the group of children were going north on Baker Street, she rode a block over to Oak. She stood up on her pedals and took off. Amy sped up Oak Street to the north end of town. She passed the last house, then turned west on Cemetery Road, heading out of town. She glanced back, but the other children still weren't in sight.

The big Goliath factory was a quarter mile down the road to the left. As she got closer to the factory, she rode past the tall chain-link fence which surrounded the factory grounds. The fence came all the way down to the road. Amy pedaled as fast as she could go.

The Centerville Cemetery was located just beyond the grounds of the factory, on the opposite side of the road. Amy slowed to a halt. An old iron-bar fence ran along the front of the cemetery and an ornate archway was spread over the entrance. Beyond the fence were rows and rows of gravestones. Some of them leaned crookedly to one side. Being there all alone made her feel creepy. She wondered how much daylight was left. The clouds above her were already turning red as the sun dropped below the horizon.

Amy decided to hide and see what was going on. She hopped off her bike and pushed it through the archway right into the cemetery. She rolled the bike between the rows of tombstones over to a large ancient oak tree. She carefully laid the bike down flat. Then she stood behind the tree and waited.

The trees in the cemetery were tall and old, like the trees at Brigadoon Farm had been. Thinking of Brigadoon Farm made her sad. In her old home, they lived on the edge of a subdivision. The back of their yard ended at the fence that surrounded the farm owned by old man Brigadoon. His farm was about the only large piece of land inside city limits that hadn't been covered with houses or stores and roads. It was like living in the country, yet still being in the city. Mr. Brigadoon and her father were friends, and he gave the Burkes permission to go on his farm.

Amy loved to walk in woods and fields, talking to her father and asking questions. Walking in the fields and woods was better than any stuffy classroom at school, Amy used to think. And she did learn a lot. Her father would identify different birds and animals and plants and trees and even rocks and minerals. They would make it like a game, seeing who could identify the most things. Sometimes they would collect water in test tubes from Raccoon Creek which ran through the farm and take it home. Then they would look at tiny drops under a microscope to see what they could see. Amy loved this kind of learning, and her father did everything he could to encourage her. Brigadoon Woods seemed like their own private paradise, a place of wonder and discovery. Nothing made her more happy than climbing over the fence with her father and crossing into Brigadoon's Farm.

Her stepmother, however, never wanted to cross the fence and enter Brigadoon Woods. She didn't like to go on walks because she had a lot of allergies and always seemed to get bitten by fleas or ticks or twist her ankle while climbing over rocks. She worried a lot when she was out in the woods. She worried about getting lost or getting poison ivy or getting bitten by snakes. She was a person who hated to get dirty, so she just stayed home. As Amy had gotten older, her stepmother took even less interest in what they discovered on their walks. She hardly ever looked in the microscope at the little drops of water. And since little Sarah's birth, her stepmother seemed totally preoccupied with the baby.

Amy understood that it took a lot of time to care for the baby. But what she didn't understand were the ways her father had been changing. For years he had seemed to make a point of spending time with Amy, either at home or in Brigadoon Woods or at a museum. But once he got his new job with Goliath Industries, things began to change. Working for Goliath had been exciting for her father. He was proud that he was making a lot more money than at his old job, and he seemed excited about the research he was doing. But he also had to work much longer hours. Amy felt forgotten. He would work late hours at the lab at the Goliath factory. And when he came home, he wasn't like his old self. He didn't seem to want to talk when Amy asked him about his work, but seemed irritated and secretive. Many evenings he would come home late, have a few bites of a warmed-up supper, then go to his library and close the door. He didn't seem to want to talk to anyone.

Amy had been puzzled and hurt by her father's change in behavior. But what was worse were the changes that had happened in Brigadoon Woods. One day Amy came home from school and heard an awful roaring noise coming from behind her house. She had run around the house in a panic. She could barely believe her eyes when she saw a huge bulldozer crashing through the trees in Brigadoon Woods. Several of the gigantic machines with big blades and tracks were ripping through the forest, toppling trees over. The trees seemed to shriek and groan as their trunks split and the roots pulled out of the ground. Amy had stood on her side of the fence and begun to cry. But she couldn't even hear herself, the noise of the machines and falling trees was so loud.

Amy was almost frantic by the time her father had gotten home that night. He looked tired. Amy wanted him to do something to make the awful machines stop tearing up their private paradise. But her father said there was nothing to be done. Like many people, especially farmers, Mr. Brigadoon had gotten in financial trouble when the depression hit. He had lost his farm to the bank and the land had been sold to be developed. Thinking better of it, her father hadn't told her that Goliath Industries were the ones who had bought the farm.

Amy had been heartbroken to see the big trees fall. She knew about the growing economic recession and the problems people were going through because she heard about it on television. And many of her friends in school in that fifth-grade year had been worried about money. But Amy's family had plenty of money, and she never thought about it. She had wanted to buy Pegasus, the old horse, but her father said they had no convenient place to keep such a large animal.

Each day when Amy came home from school, less and less was left of Brigadoon Woods. The big machines seemed like angry giant insects, tearing up whatever was in their path. Within two weeks, all that was left was raw bare land, full of tractor tracks and pieces of roots sticking up from the ground. Raccoon Creek was like a muddy ditch. Even the old man Brigadoon's farmhouse was bulldozed flat. That night her father came home and announced that they were moving. Goliath Industries had transferred them to a place called Centerville. Amy was almost relieved that they would be moving. She didn't think she could bear to watch them change Brigadoon Woods even more.

Amy woke up from her daydream about Brigadoon Farm when she heard voices. Several children on bikes came into view far down the road. They were talking loudly as they pedaled past the field of graves. Amy peeked from behind the tree trunk. Sloan and the other children stopped at the corner of the land just west of the cemetery. They all got off their bikes and parked them, except Tiffany.

Tiffany was holding the handlebars of a rather large old red bike. She pushed the bike out into a sparsely wooded field as the other children followed. When Amy felt that it was safe, she ran down a row of gravestones and climbed over the cemetery fence to follow the other children.

Amy crouched down and scurried over to a nearby tree. The sky was getting darker more quickly than she had anticipated. She began to wonder if she should have come on this wild-goose chase. She didn't want to be caught in the dark so far from home. She was thinking of just getting her bike and sneaking away when she heard laughter. She decided to get closer, running from tree to tree until she came upon the children.

The group was gathered in a half circle. In front of them was the bike Tiffany had been pushing. Amy scooted through some tall weeds to get even closer. She kept going until she stopped behind a large bushy tree only fifteen feet away. From that distance she could see all the children more clearly. She recognized each face from school though she didn't know all of their names.

Then she looked at the bike. It was something of an oddity since it was an old red bicycle with big balloon tires. Amy had seen bikes like that in photographs before, but it clearly wasn't like most thin, modern ten-speeds or rugged dirt bikes. There was some white writing on the middle bar. She squinted her eyes and made out the words *Spirit Flyer*.

Then Amy noticed something else. The old red bike was parked on top of a real dark place. She had assumed it was just a shadow at first, but it looked too dark. Besides that, it was in the exact shape of a long dark rectangle. The dark thing seemed to be hard, like a panel of glass or plastic. Both balloon tires of the old bicycle were resting directly on top of the rectangle.

"This is the right spot," Sloan said, setting the gas can on the ground. "We just need to wait until it gets darker. Then we'll offer the sacrifice."

One of the children turned on a flashlight. Amy had a nagging feeling that she should leave, but she was too curious. The children in the group talked quietly among themselves as the darkness fell.

"How did you get permission to get the bike?" a girl asked Tiffany.

"Well, Lawrence is new in town, and he doesn't want to be Rank Blank on the Big Board," Tiffany said. "And since the school got its own Big Board yesterday, he was really desperate to get a rank. I told Lawrence that if he'd let me borrow his bike for a test drive, then he could qualify for a rank in the Point System. I told him I would only use the bike for an hour. Our time is almost up."

"Uncle Bunkie said we needed to sacrifice a Spirit Flyer to get the field ready for the games," Sloan said. "Stand back. I'm not sure what's supposed to happen. These Spirit Flyer bikes can be tricky."

The other children moved away from the bike in the direction of the road. Sloan picked up the gas can and held it over his head.

"For Caves and Cobras," Sloan announced. "With fire, let the games begin." The blond-headed boy then began sloshing gasoline all over the old red bicycle. Amy thought she could hear a hissing sound, like water hitting a hot skillet. Sloan emptied the can. Then he stepped backward and handed the can to one of the other boys.

"Stand back!" Sloan yelled over his shoulder. The other children moved farther into the shadows. Sloan took a box of wooden kitchen matches from a bag. He struck one match and watched it flare. Then with a flick of his wrist, he tossed it toward the bike.

It all happened in a flash and a whoosh. Amy jumped back as the gasoline loudly exploded into a blaze. Then came another terrible

wrenching sound. A roar and rumbling filled the air so loudly that the ground shook. She heard one of the children scream. Other voices could be heard above the roaring noise.

"It's an earthquake!"

And indeed it seemed that way to Amy. She fell to her knees as the ground churned beneath her feet. The ground was moving so much that she felt like she was in a rowboat out in the middle of the ocean. The fire flared up into the darkening sky as a tree toppled and fell into the flames. The rumbling roar of the ground and crackling fire seemed deafening. Voices were yelling off in the darkness. Amy tried to run back toward the cemetery, but she fell down again. The whole world seemed to be shaking. A tree fell to the ground right beside her. A large branch pinned her legs. Amy struggled to free herself, but the branch was too heavy. The ground seemed to be breaking up all around her.

Then suddenly, the shaking stopped. The earthquake was over, but the fire had just begun.

A VISIT
TO THE
KINGDOM

3

The whole night seemed to be on fire to Amy. She wiggled her legs, but the heavy limbs of the fallen tree still held her. A wind blew the flames toward the girl. The fire raced through the dry brushy weeds and then jumped into the tree that had trapped her. Amy screamed as the fire began eating the branches, crackling and snapping up the browned autumn leaves.

With a rush of wind, hot smoke covered the girl. Her eyes burned as she coughed. She screamed out again, pulling her legs frantically. But the heavy tree limbs wouldn't let go. The orange flames shot high into the sky.

Amy yelled once more. Through the smoke, she saw a bright light high above her, shining like a powerful spotlight. But this light had to be at least thirty feet in the air. Suddenly, the light fell right on her face. Amy yelled out, waving her arms. "Help me!" she shouted. Then she began coughing. The light seemed to fall from the sky. The smoke was so thick, Amy wasn't sure quite what happened next. Suddenly there was a boy in jeans and a t-shirt standing next to her. He bent over and lifted the tree limb.

"Pull your legs out!" he shouted. His face seemed orange in the glow of the fire. The boy looked very familiar, but the flickering firelight and hot smoke confused the girl. Amy felt the weight of the tree branches lessen. She braced herself with her arms and pulled back. Her legs sprang free.

"Follow me!" the boy shouted. He pulled Amy toward a bright light about ten feet away. As they got closer, Amy saw a large old bicycle with big balloon tires. A headlight fastened to the handlebars was turned on. The boy hopped on the seat. "Get on the back and hang on!" the boy shouted. Amy moved quickly. She held onto his waist as the bike began to move. At first Amy was surprised that they were riding across the ground without feeling any bumps; the ride seemed unusually smooth. But she was even more surprised as the bicycle shot right into the air.

Amy yelped and lurched forward, holding onto the boy's waist with all her might. For an instant, she thought they had shot off a hill and would begin falling any second. But the big bicycle didn't come down. They just went higher and higher into the night air, as if they were flying. Amy looked down. The fire burning below gave enough light for her to see that they were already higher than the highest tree. The bicycle was flying!

"What's happening?" Amy shouted. She suddenly felt afraid again and very confused.

"Just hang on," the boy said over his shoulder. "You're ok, now."

Amy wasn't sure that was true at all as she looked down at the fire below. She wondered if she were having a nightmare. Then she looked toward town. Through the rising clouds of smoke, the lights of Centerville were twinkling in the distance. Then off to the left, two lights were approaching like the headlights of a car. Amy's mouth dropped open when she saw two more children on bicycles zoom up beside them, high in the middle of the sky. One was a boy and the other was a girl. Amy shook her head, thinking she must be imagining things. All three of the bicycles had come to a total stop, yet they had to be at least a hundred feet off the ground.

"Did you see Larry's bike?" the girl asked.

"No," the boy in front of Amy said. "We were too late."

"Let's get out of this smoke," the other boy said. The bicycle riders turned in the air. Amy got a better grip on the boy's waist as they shot forward through the sky.

"Stay away from the factory," the girl bike rider called out. Amy looked down at the Goliath factory as the bicycles made a long slow turn, going south of the big smokestacks. They passed directly over the grounds of the newly opened Goliath Country Club as they flew.

As they got closer to town, the bikes dropped closer to the ground. They were only a few feet above the ground when they reached the west end of Tenth Street. As they passed the first street light, all three bikes touched down on the pavement. The minute the wheels hit the ground, Amy jumped off. The fear about the earthquake and fire and strange flying bicycles had filled the girl with growing panic. She began running as fast she could toward the center of town.

"Hey, wait up!" she heard a boy's voice call. Amy just sped up. Even though she was a good runner, she couldn't outrun the bicycles for very long. Off to her left she saw a redheaded boy on a bicycle pedaling up closer. She looked over and could have sworn the big balloon tires of the bike were at least three inches off the pavement.

"We're your friends," the boy called to her.

Amy just ran harder. The town square was only half a block away.

"I think the kings have something to show her," the boy with red hair called, looking over to the others who had pulled up alongside Amy on her right. They nodded. Without speaking, they all reached down and pushed the gear levers forward.

The lights of the old bikes brightened with the sound of a whoosh, like a sudden gust of wind. Amy could even feel it shooting by her. Then it happened, right before her eyes. The three beams of light from the old bicycles seemed to twist together and grow more narrow instead of spreading out. Amy slowed down as a long vertical white line suddenly appeared, almost like a bolt of lightning right in the middle of the town square. Only this line of light didn't disappear but hung there in the air, going right down into the street. The sky seemed to rumble as the crack of light suddenly began to grow. Amy stopped running. She stood in the street, staring. Her mouth hung open as she watched in amazement the scene unfolding before her.

The crack of light had grown wider, first as wide as a door, then as wide as the street. The scene before Amy's eyes began to change. Though Amy knew it was night, the scene before her was as bright as the brightest day she had ever seen. She rubbed her eyes and looked again. The three children were stopped beside her, the lights on their bicycles still turned on. The crack kept getting wider and wider until there was nothing left at all before her but the brightly lit place.

Amy whirled around in a circle. It was as if the whole world had been divided in half. Behind her was the night, but spread out before her was like the dawning of a brand new day in a brand new time. She looked down. The bright light came all the way up to her toes, then stopped. Just looking into the mysterious scene before her made Amy's heart leap with a kind of bubbly joy. She suddenly felt as if she could jump thirty feet up in the air without even trying. Her doubts about the recent escape from the fire and the strange bicycle ride were quickly forgotten. She sensed she was on the edge of a paradise she had never known before. She thought of Brigadoon Farm, but this was more than a hundred Brigadoon Farms put together. Amy wanted to say something as she looked into the wonders before her, but she found she couldn't speak.

"We're there," the boy who rescued her said. He looked at Amy with a smile.

Amy looked ahead. She still seemed to be in Centerville, but it was a Centerville almost beyond description, as if there were much more in and around and through than she had ever imagined. Things seemed to be at a great distance, as if she were looking into a place beyond time, a place with no end or boundaries. Though the light was very bright, it wasn't like ordinary daylight. The light seemed to have something extra in it, as if flavored with honey.

"Daylight flavored like honey?" Amy said softly. "That doesn't make any sense."

"That's a good way to describe it," a girl next to her said. "Welcome to the Kingdom of the Three Kings. Of course, this is only a glimpse."

"Where are we? What happened?" Amy asked. "Am I dreaming? Did I die in the fire? If I'm dead, it feels very peaceful and nice."

"You didn't die," the boy who had rescued her said. "You're just near the life of the kingdom and the peace of the presence of the kings." The other children looked at her and smiled. Amy recognized all the children from school. The boy who had rescued her was in her class at school. He was named John. The other children were in the class ahead of her. She wasn't sure of their names.

"I'm John Kramar," said the boy.

"I know. We're in the same class," Amy said. "I'm Amy Burke. Thanks for . . . uh . . . helping me out back there."

"And I'm Susan Kramar," the girl said. She smiled. "John is my cousin."

"And I'm Daniel Bayley," the redheaded boy said.

Amy nodded, then looked back into the brightness. "Where are we?" Amy asked softly.

"We're still in Centerville," John said. "But the kingdom is here, only it's Deeper. It's not always this strong, but the kings must have wanted you to see it."

"But can this be?" Amy asked, staring straight ahead into the wonder. "I see the town too, but everything has changed."

"It's like looking deeper into another dimension, sort of," Daniel said. "That's why they call it the Deeper World, only there's more to the Deeper World than the kingdom."

"More?" Amy asked in surprise. She felt like she hadn't even begun to see what she was looking at. The place before her seemed to call her. She wanted to run right in, and she wasn't sure why she didn't. That's when she thought she heard someone call her name.

"He's here," John Kramar said. Amy looked at her rescuer. He was smiling as he looked into the brightness. The other children were looking too. Amy turned to see what they were staring at when she saw him.

Off in the distance was someone who looked like a man, but Amy knew right away he was more than a man. If possible, he was brighter than the other lights. Amy stared in awe at this figure. No words could describe how she felt. All Amy knew was that he had called out her name. He knew her name and something about that fact made her suddenly feel new and different, as if she had suddenly grown three inches. "Who is he?" Amy barely whispered.

"That's the Prince of Kings," John said. "And he's calling you to come to him."

Amy stood on the edge between two worlds. The wonderful, strange prince came closer. His eyes looked so kind and wise and inviting. She took a small step into the light, then took another step until she was half in and half out.

Suddenly things changed. A great heaviness came upon the girl. "What's happening?" Amy cried out in fear. She looked down. That's when she saw the chain. A long dark chain was hanging down her chest. And around her neck was a large metal ring. The dark chain was attached to the ring with an oddly shaped lock of a kind that Amy had never seen before. In the center of the lock was a circle with an X inside. As Amy stared at the circled X, a bolt of fear shot through her body. She suddenly felt very afraid and sad deep within herself. She felt trapped, like a slave. The chain ran from her body and out into the world from where she had just come. But she couldn't see where it ended. She took another step toward the glowing figure when she felt the chain pull tight.

"I can't go any farther," Amy cried out, looking down at the chain. Amy yanked on the chain to pull it off. The heavy dark links felt dead cold in her hands. Something about it seemed very evil. No matter how hard she yanked, she only rattled the chain. The lock remained shut. Though the chain just seemed to disappear into thin air, it seemed attached to something on the other end as she pulled.

"I don't like this," Amy blurted out. "Make it stop. Please make it stop."

"It's the chain that holds you back," John Kramar said. "But you don't have to be a slave to it anymore. In the kingdom you can be free. The Prince of Kings has given us keys to unlock the locks. Look in your hand."

Amy looked down. She was startled to see a flat golden metal object shaped like a key. Most keys had cuts and grooves, but this key was flat and smooth. At the top of the key were some marks. Stamped in the golden metal were three small crowns.

"The key is a free gift. Use it and enter the kingdom," Susan said.

Amy looked at the key and then looked back at the Prince of Kings. Suddenly she realized that she could go toward him by unlocking the chain. But at the same time, she realized something deeper. Without anyone telling her, she knew deep inside that if you are in the presence of a king, you bow down before him. At that moment, the chain began pulling her back toward the darkness.

"Free yourself!" John cried. "You don't have to be a slave anymore."

But Amy hesitated, thinking of what it meant to bow down before a king. Perhaps it was her stubborn streak. All she could think of suddenly was that she didn't like the idea of bowing down to anyone. Deep inside she felt torn in two directions. Part of her wanted to run into the arms of the king, no matter what it meant. Yet another part of her held back. As she resisted, the weight of the chain seemed even heavier. Then, before she knew it, she was dragged out of the light back into the darkness.

She shuddered as the light behind her quivered and then suddenly started to dim. The chain began fading around her neck. Within a minute, everything was back to normal. She was in the town square of Centerville on a Friday evening. The lights on the big red bicycles had gone off. The other children looked at Amy sadly.

Amy looked down at her right hand. The key was gone. She looked back to where she had seen the glowing figure, the one they called the Prince of Kings. He was gone too, though something about his presence seemed to linger in the air.

"I must be dreaming or something," Amy said shaking her head. "You guys are trying to trick me. Something very strange is going on tonight and I don't like it."

Amy stared at the old red bicycles like they were objects from outer space. Each bike seemed to be more or less like the other one. They all had the same name: *Spirit Flyer.*

"Spirit Flyers are pretty special bicycles," Susan said. "We have a friend named Lawrence who let someone borrow his Spirit Flyer bike. Only they tricked him."

"I saw a bike like that out there," Amy said. "Why would they want to burn it? They poured a can of gasoline on it and lit a match. That's how the fire started. Then the whole field began moving and rocking like an earthquake. I've never been so scared in my life."

"You mean you weren't helping them?" Susan asked.

"No," Amy said. "I live next door to Sloan and Tiffany in Buckingham

Estates. I overheard them talking and knew they were up to something. They were acting real secretive about it. I followed them into the field, but they didn't see me. I still don't know what's going on. They said something about a game."

Amy looked suspiciously at the other children. She reached up and felt around her neck, wondering if she would find the chain. Though she couldn't touch it, the bad feeling she had when she had seen it was still all over her.

"Maybe I bumped my head when I fell down," Amy mumbled softly as she touched her head.

"Why didn't you use the key?" John Kramar asked. "You could have been free from the chain. You didn't have to be a slave anymore."

"I'm just as free as anyone else," Amy said, stepping backward, away from the other children. "You guys are just trying to trick me somehow. I don't know how you do it, but it must be a trick."

"We can explain some of the kingdom," Daniel Bayley said softly. "I know it's strange. The first time I saw the kingdom and the Kingson, I was really confused. But once you get to know him and the kingdom, you realize how—"

Just then, a loud siren began to blow all over town. Amy jumped up in fear. She looked up at the sky as if it were about to fall. Then without a word, she took off running.

"Wait!" John Kramar yelled after her. "That's just the fire horn blowing to call the volunteers. They must have spotted the fire out by the cemetery."

But Amy wasn't listening. She ran as if she was being chased, but when she looked over her shoulder, she saw no one. The children on the old red bicycles weren't following her. Amy ran and ran, from block to block, from street light to street light. A great heaviness seemed to be all over her. And it wouldn't leave her, no matter how fast she ran.

Back in her room, she finally felt safe, though the heavy feeling wouldn't leave her. She had trouble falling asleep. She lay in her bed, thinking of all the strange events of that evening. She touched her neck often, feeling for the chain. But all she felt was a vague sort of fear deep inside herself. She finally fell asleep, pulled into the restless dark of dreams.

BICYCLE
HILLS

· · · · · · · ·

4

Amy woke up on Saturday morning, and the first thing she noticed was a faint odor of smoke in her room. The clothes she had worn the night before were sitting on a chair next to her bed. They smelled of smoke. She quickly ran to her dresser. She faced the mirror and touched her neck. Her reflection didn't reveal anything unusual. In the first hazy moments of waking up, she had been wondering if the night before could have been some kind of nightmare. But a dream wouldn't explain the smoky smell in her clothes.

After she dressed, she picked up the smoky clothes. Her black number card fell out of her pocket onto the carpet. As Amy bent down, something golden and shiny fell out of her shirt pocket and landed a quarter of an inch away from the number card. Amy reached down, then stopped, staring as if she were looking at a ghost. The odd-shaped golden key with the three crowns glinted up at her. She stared at it for a long moment. Once again she felt in turmoil, pulled in different directions deep inside. She looked at her dark face shining up at her from the number card. Then she looked at a golden reflection of her face in the key.

Amy reached for the golden key and then stopped. She looked at the number card. Suddenly, with a quick motion, Amy kicked the golden key under her bed, out of sight. She picked up the dark little number card and put it in her back pocket. She bent down to look under the bed. The key was still there. Amy pulled the bedspread all the way down to the floor, as if to hide the golden key. Something about it made her uneasy, but she didn't really want to throw it away.

She stood and walked out of her room down to the kitchen. On Saturday mornings, she usually fixed breakfast for herself. She ate a quick bowl of cereal and then went looking for her father. Her step-mother was in the living room changing the baby's diaper.

"Where's Dad?" Amy asked.

"In his study."

Amy ran upstairs to his study. She didn't bother to knock on the door. She walked in and found him sitting at his desk. He was looking down at a small black box about seven inches square. The box was made of a shiny material, perhaps black glass or plastic. And on one side was a curious marking: a white X inside a white circle. Something about the sight of the circled X made Amy feel funny.

"What's that?" Amy asked. Her father jumped, as if startled. He quickly covered the black box with a folded newspaper.

"I didn't hear you come in," he said. Her father looked tired and worn out even though it was early in the morning. He also seemed nervous, Amy thought.

"I was wondering if we could go on a walk today," Amy said. "There's a river they call the Sleepy Eye near town, and we could collect some samples and use the microscopes."

"Not today," her father said. He stood up. "I've got to work today."

"But you promised we'd go on a walk," Amy whined. "We haven't done anything together since we moved here."

"I know it, Honey," her father said. He looked sad. "But I just don't have time. We'll go on a walk soon though. I promise."

"But that's what you promised last Saturday," Amy said with a pout. She knew it was useless to argue. Without another word, she turned and stomped out of the study. She was extra loud on the stairs. Amy felt betrayed. Her father had broken another promise. For a moment she wanted to just scream and wished she didn't live in a world with adults who didn't keep promises or who were picky, like her stepmother. And while she was at it, she would eliminate all teachers and principals and just everyone. Amy stomped outside and slammed the front door behind her.

Though it was still fairly early in the morning, a lot of children seemed to be outside that day. Across the street a bunch of boys were on their bicycles, parked in front of the garage at the Smedlowe house. Mr. Smedlowe was the school principal at Centerville. The Smedlowes had a son named Barry who was in Amy's class. Though she didn't know Barry very well, she knew he was the leader of a group of boys called the Cobra Club. Barry and the other boys in the club took off on their bikes.

They had just turned the corner when Amy heard voices over at the Favor's fancy big house. Amy watched Tiffany and Sloan Favor roll their bikes out of the garage and down the driveway. They hopped on and coasted out into the street. As soon as they turned the corner, Amy remembered that she had left her own bicycle at the cemetery.

Amy walked and ran over the same route she had taken the night before. When she got close to the cemetery, she wasn't that surprised to see all the shiny bicycles parked by the field. News traveled fast in Centerville, and it seemed over a hundred children had gathered to look at the fire's damage.

But as Amy got closer, she was surprised at what she saw. The whole landscape had changed. A huge area, about the size of a football field, was cleared out and blackened from the fire. But what seemed really different were all the small hills. Amy was sure the hills hadn't been there the night before. But all over the field were hills of various sizes. Some were probably up to ten feet high. One hill in the center of the field was higher than all the rest. And standing on the top of that hill was Sloan Favor. Hands on his hips, he stood erect like a general. His blue eyes surveyed the burnt ruins that looked like a battlefield. Tiffany and some other kids were standing next to him.

Amy went through the archway into the cemetery. Her bike was just where she had left it. She picked it up and rolled it out to the road. She pedaled the short distance to the burnt field and parked her bike among the other bicycles.

Amy walked into the field of hills, carefully stepping among the ashes and muddy puddles left by the firemen's water. Smoke drifted up from a fallen burnt tree trunk lying sideways on the ground. The whole place smelled of smoke and tar. But there was another smell, a slight odor that smelled as if something had died. Amy sniffed the air and coughed.

Children were gathered in groups. Amy carefully looked around the field. As she figured it, the hill where Sloan was standing was just about the same place where he had poured gasoline on the bicycle the night before. She wondered how all the hills had appeared so quickly. Then she remembered the earthquake. Perhaps the hills had been pushed up out of the ground. But she thought it was odd that only this one field should be affected. Nothing else in the cemetery or in town or anywhere else seemed to have been disturbed by the earthquake, if it was an earthquake.

Amy wandered toward the larger hill. Barry Smedlowe and his club had gathered around and seemed to be yelling at Sloan. No one seemed to notice as Amy got closer.

"We beat you fair and square, Smedlowe," Sloan said.

"You cheated and you know it," Barry whined.

"But what happened to the bike?" a boy named Wilbur asked. "My dad is the fire chief, and he said they didn't find anything out here. It couldn't have just burned up into nothing."

"It didn't burn up at all, I don't think," Tiffany said softly. "After we got back in town, I went to see Lawrence. The bike was parked in the driveway. I about swallowed my gum when I saw it. The tires were flat and Lawrence blamed me. He said he came outside and found it that way. He was really mad and kind of scared. Those Rank Blank Kramar kids and Daniel Bayley were there too."

"But it couldn't have been the same bike," Wilbur said. "How did it get there?"

"I told you before that those bikes are tricky," Sloan said. He grinned, but it wasn't a happy grin, Amy thought. "The main thing is that our club sacrificed a Spirit Flyer first. We're points ahead on the Big Board now for sure. I'm Number One in this town, and I aim to stay that way."

"Only because you cheated," Barry yelled out.

"You're just a sore loser," Sloan said. "And once the games get going, we'll knock you down to the rank you deserve. We'll be the only ones in town to qualify for the Trag 7 power units. And once we get those, nothing can stop us. Look! Here comes Uncle Bunkie! Maybe we can start the games today."

The children cheered and ran down the charred hill. Amy ran to join the crowd of children gathering at the road. A small black truck had parked in front of the burned field. A sign was painted on the side of the truck: *Goliath Toys, Giants of Fun Fun Fun!!!* Suddenly, the back doors of the truck opened and out came the smiling face of a clown!

"Hey, kids!" the clown shouted out.

"Hey, Uncle Bunkie!" the children shouted back.

Uncle Bunkie the clown pulled a ramp down the back of the truck. Then he walked down it, his big oversized clown shoes slapping along. He was carrying a purple plastic bucket in each hand. Uncle Bunkie had a stringy mop of wild orange hair and a big red ball on his nose. He also had a white painted face with a red painted grin as big as a banana. His bright baggy clothes were covered with polka dots. When he got to the bottom of the ramp, he acted like he tripped and was going to spill his buckets. All the children roared with laughter.

Amy knew Uncle Bunkie had been the manager of the toy store for about a month. He was supposedly related to an old woman named Mrs. Happy who had run the store before. But she had mysteriously disappeared the day school started. Uncle Bunkie arrived in town just two days later.

All the children liked him, especially the little ones because he was always dressed up like a clown, even in the store. Sometimes he changed into different costumes, but you could still tell it was Uncle Bunkie because of his voice. He had a pleasant, bouncy voice. Some children said they had seen Uncle Bunkie on television before. They claimed he used to be the host of a program where they would show cartoons and play games with children.

Uncle Bunkie turned to walk back up the ramp into the back of the truck, but he pretended to trip again. The children howled. Amy laughed too because Uncle Bunkie looked so goofy. She ran over to join the crowd.

Tiffany and Sloan and the other children surrounded the big clown. He gave a bucket to Sloan and one to Tiffany. The purple buckets were full of little candies in paper wrappers. The other children eagerly reached into the buckets and grabbed handfuls. Amy moved closer and got a handful of candy from Tiffany. The writing on the wrappers said *Rainbow Dream Drops.* The candies were flat and round, about the size of a penny. A spiral of rainbow colors started from the center of the candy and spread to the edges. Like everyone else, Amy popped a few of the candies into her mouth and stuffed the rest in her pockets.

The flavor was hard to describe because it kept changing. At first it seemed like mint, but then it tasted fruity, then sour, then sweet. Then there was an unpleasant medicine flavor, like an awful cough drop. Amy felt a rushing dizzy feeling that made her shudder. She was about to spit the candies out, when the bad flavor was suddenly replaced by a sweet cherry taste, then mint again. The flavors kept changing, but the medicine taste didn't return.

Uncle Bunkie walked back up the ramp into the truck. When he returned, he was pushing a flashy golden ten-speed. A gasp went up from the children. Like every other child, Amy stepped closer for a better look.

At first she didn't see what was so special. The bicycle was a Goliath Super Wings, the best bike Goliath made. Amy had seen Super Wings before, but she had never seen one with so many attachments on the handlebars. Right in the middle of the handlebars was a black box about seven inches square. The dark sides were shiny, as if they were made of black plastic or glass. And on the side facing the rider was a curious white marking—a white X inside a white circle.

Something about the box and the circled X seemed familiar and made her uneasy. Then she remembered—the box on the bicycle looked identical to the box her father had on his desk, the box he had been so secretive about that morning. The circled X had been on the lock and chain she had seen the night before when she had stepped into the strange lighted place.

Amy was so busy staring at the circled X that she hardly noticed the three big tractor-trailer trucks that pulled up and parked in front of the burnt field. Several men in gray uniforms got out of the trucks. The men moved quickly to the rear of one of the trailers and began unloading some tall metal poles. Other men took the poles and tilted them into a series of concrete holes that were already in place. They were about ten feet apart and ran in a straight line down the front border of the field parallel to Cemetery Road. Two men set the poles and bolted them down with two big bolts.

Uncle Bunkie pushed the bike into the burnt, muddy field. Like all the other children, Amy was right behind him. Besides the bike, the funny clown carried a brown paper bag under his arm. He kept pushing until he was at the foot of the highest hill among the field of hills. Then with surprisingly little effort, he pushed the shiny golden bicycle to the top of the hill. He knocked down the kickstand and let the bike rest.

"Hey, kids, guess what? A new game is coming to town!" Uncle Bunkie shouted. The children cheered and laughed. Uncle Bunkie's red nose glowed on and off like a light bulb. That made the kids laugh even louder. The clown waited until the noise stopped. "As many of you already know, the game is called Caves and Cobras," said Uncle Bunkie. "We also call it C & C or the Double C game. There have been rumors about starting the game all fall. But now the time and place is right, thanks to the help of Sloan Favor and his club called the Super Wings."

Tiffany and Sloan Favor clapped their hands while their friends cheered. But not all the children were happy, Amy noticed. Barry Smedlowe and the Cobra Club booed loudly. Uncle Bunkie waited for quiet.

"Before I demonstrate the treasure to be won by playing the game, we must make one thing clear," Uncle Bunkie said in a suddenly solemn voice. "For the moment, these games must be kept an absolute secret. In fact, everything that goes on within the boundaries of this field must be secret. That is why those men are building a special privacy wall." The children looked back toward the road. The men were moving quickly. Several poles were already standing along the front of the field.

"Once the privacy wall is done, the games can begin. These are special games for you special children. No adults are allowed. So no one, and I mean no one, can whisper a word about this to any person who doesn't qualify for the game. If you tell, the fun will be spoiled."

"Not even our parents can know?" Barry Smedlowe asked with a grin.

"Especially not them," said the clown. "If you tell, your team will lose points and maybe the game itself. Then you may miss out on having a Trag 7 power unit for your bicycle."

"But why can't we tell any adults?" Amy blurted out. She felt embarrassed when the clown stared at her silently for a moment. His eyes almost looked angry.

"If you want to play, you play by my rules," Uncle Bunkie said. Then the twinkle came back into his eyes. "The reason has to do with what we call product development. And besides, the games are to be kept a secret only for a short time. Halloween is coming up in just a few weeks. The first round of games will be over by then and the winners will be announced. That's the new target date."

The children smiled and whispered among themselves. They popped more candies into their mouths. Many children liked the idea of having a special game that was a secret from their parents.

"I don't think your parents would worry even if they did know about Caves and Cobras," Uncle Bunkie said. "After all, it's a friendly secret. As you know, there are many toys an adult wouldn't want to play with. In the same way, this is a game for children. The grownups in Centerville have their own games and toys. Goliath Industries just finished the new country club for them. They can have fun over there."

"But what will we tell them we're doing when we play the game?" Sloan asked.

"I'm sure you can think of something that won't make them suspicious," the clown replied with an enormous smile. "Just tell them you're having fun out at Bicycle Hills."

"Bicycle Hills," the children all whispered to themselves. For some reason, the name had an almost enchanting ring to it. Like the others, Amy said it softly to herself. Then she pulled more candies out of her pocket. Amy didn't normally have much of a sweet tooth, but the combined flavors of the Dream Drops seemed irresistible. She unwrapped two more and placed them on her tongue to melt.

"Now let me give a short demonstration of the Trag 7 power unit," the clown said with his bouncy voice.

Amy watched carefully as the clown got on the bicycle. He reached into the paper bag he was holding and pulled something out. Amy thought she heard a chirping noise. Uncle Bunkie took whatever was in his hand and pushed it up against the side of the black box with the white circled X. There was a hissing sound at first and then silence. The clown's hand was suddenly empty.

"Now for the ride," Uncle Bunkie said with his enormous red smile. He pushed the kickstand of the Super Wings up with his long black shoes and rolled the bike forward. Amy wasn't surprised to see the golden bicycle roll down the hill, but it seemed to be rolling unusually fast. It zipped right up the next hill so quickly that it sailed right out into the air, as if shot off a ramp. And the bicycle just kept going. The children gasped at how high and fast the bicycle traveled. They watched with their eyes filled with wonder. Like everyone else, Amy was curious to see how far the bike could go before dropping, but the golden Super Wings just went higher into the sky.

"It's not coming down!" Sloan yelled out. "I knew it. Watch it fly!"

And it was true. For the second time in two days, Amy was seeing a bicycle doing something she couldn't explain. Like everyone else, she watched in awe as the golden bicycle seemed to break all the rules of gravity. Amy popped two more candies in her mouth as the Goliath Super Wings flew higher and higher above the burnt mounds of dirt called Bicycle Hills. When the children began to cheer and clap their hands, Amy joined in the celebration.

THE
WALLS
GO UP
· · · · · · · · ·

5

The children watched with open mouths as the golden Super Wings bicycle shot out over the sea of hills. Uncle Bunkie the clown leveled the bike off at about fifty feet above the ground. He turned in a circle and then zoomed toward the crowd of children.

Amy blinked and rubbed her eyes as the clown on the shiny bicycle sailed right over her head. The children on the ground cheered wildly, clapping their hands together. Uncle Bunkie flew all the way to the edge of the field by the cemetery before circling back. As he got closer, the bicycle dropped toward the ground. On a flat place between two small

hills, the bike touched down on the dirt. Then the golden bicycle shot up a hill and into the air. Uncle Bunkie smiled as he sailed completely over the next hill and landed in the valley below. His funny orange hair blew in the breeze as the bike sped along.

The children were amazed as the clown on the bike rode around the field in a large sort of circle. He would zoom up one hill, then fly completely over the next two hills, then land on the flat ground beyond. He made a complete circle around the field and started off again. But he hadn't ridden far when he turned sharply in toward the center of the field. He shot off a hill in front of the children and sailed over their heads, not hitting the ground again until he was past the tallest hill.

"Hey, kids! Follow me!" Uncle Bunkie shouted as he flew over their upturned faces. No one had to be told twice. There was an immediate stampede toward the group of bicycles parked out by Cemetery Road. Amy rushed along with the crowd.

Sloan Favor jumped on his Goliath Super Wings bike and took off. He quickly pulled out in front of the others as he shot up a hill. Amy and the other children were close behind. Amy shot up the first hill. Her bicycle jumped a few feet in the air, but then came back down normally. No one's bike was performing like the fully equipped Super Wings that Uncle Bunkie was riding. But the children didn't seem to care. The funny clown slowed down so they could follow him. They rode around and around Bicycle Hills in a large circle that soon looked like a race track for dirt bikes. Besides the long circle around the field, two diagonal tracks were formed across the field like a large X. The diagonal paths met right at the top of the tallest hill in the center of the field.

Boys and girls on bikes zoomed over the dirt hills at a dizzying speed. Amy rode her bicycle as fast as she could go. Before long, her face was red and hot from all the pedaling. Riding up and down and over the hills and valleys was more fun than she had imagined. Amy, like the other children, seemed to lose track of time as they sped up and down the hills.

No one noticed at first, but Uncle Bunkie had finally stopped riding after about fifteen minutes. The clown parked near the center hill. He stood beside the Super Wings and smiled his enormous red smile as he watched the children having fun. He pressed the center of the X in the circle while putting his hand under the box. A gray powder that looked like ashes dropped from the bottom of the box into his hand. He scooped the powder up into his mouth and swallowed it with one gulp.

While the children continued riding, Uncle Bunkie pushed the Super Wings bicycle back to the black truck parked at the front of the field. He rolled the golden bicycle up the ramp into the back of the truck. He put away the ramp. Then looking to see if any of the children were watching, he stepped inside the truck and locked the doors.

The clown moved toward the front of the truck. A thin old man sat in the front passenger seat. He was holding a plastic bucket full of Rainbow Dream Drops. "Good job," the old man said. "You set the hooks well. Every kid in town will be demanding a Trag 7 and they'll do anything to get one. You'll be rewarded properly if you do this job right."

"Thanks, Mr. Cutright," Uncle Bunkie said. His big red grin seemed enormous. "They really seem to like the candy."

"Of course they do," the old man replied. "You keep the dosage low and it builds up in their system, slow and steady, like sweet poison. By Halloween, they'll be just right: hungry and eager enough to be re-moved. The little idiots will do anything for pleasure and escape, and we'll help them make that escape . . . so they never return."

The old man chuckled as Uncle Bunkie grinned his enormous red smile. Then the clown stopped smiling. "But what about the Spirit Flyer kids?" Uncle Bunkie asked. "They worry me."

"Well, it's true they're increasing in number," Mr. Cutright said. "That fool Mrs. Happy really goofed up the operation last month. We lost the Bayley boy and at least nine or more others in just a few weeks."

"And last night they were tempting the Burke girl," Uncle Bunkie said.

"Well, we must contain the damage," the old man said. "You know what to do. Now get back out there with those brats. By Halloween, I want this town cleaned up. We can't be the only ones behind when the final campaign starts."

The old man handed Uncle Bunkie the purple bucket of Dream Drops. The clown took them and smiled. He turned and honked the horn on the black truck three times. Uncle Bunkie opened the door and waved for the children to come see him. The children on bicycles came from all directions, speeding up and down the hills. Amy joined the crowd. As Uncle Bunkie handed out the buckets of candy, the children grabbed desperately for it. The clown smiled.

"As I mentioned before, the games can't begin until the walls go up," Uncle Bunkie said, standing on the rear bumper of the truck. "Much of the work has already been prepared, so the wall should be done by this afternoon around three o'clock. If you want to see if you qualify for the game of Caves and Cobras, meet me back out here at that time. I'll explain the rules and some of the equipment you may want to use. So until then, Bicycle Hills is closed."

Disappointment covered the red sweaty faces of the children as they slowly pedaled their bicycles out to Cemetery Road. Amy moved along with the crowd, trying not to get run over. But as the others pedaled back toward town, Amy paused to watch Uncle Bunkie talk to the men working on the privacy walls. Two of the men went into the back of one of the trailers and returned carrying a long black rectangle about seven feet high and ten feet long. The panel looked something like a window made of black glass or plastic. A thin dark casing ran around the edges of the panel like a frame.

The men carried the panel over to the row of metal poles. As Uncle Bunkie instructed them, they carefully placed the panel between two poles. The bottom edge rested on the ground. The men took long bolts from their work belts and stuck them through the panels into the poles.

They put three such bolts in each side. Then they went back to the truck and returned with the next dark shiny panel. Amy was surprised how quickly the panels were set in place.

Uncle Bunkie looked over at Amy, then walked toward her. Amy looked behind her. All of the other children were gone. "Bicycle Hills is closed for now, young lady," Uncle Bunkie said. Even his painted-on smile wasn't smiling.

"I was just watching them put up the wall," Amy replied.

"It looked like you were snooping," the clown said firmly. "And snooping children can get in trouble. In fact, I know about a snooping little girl who almost got in serious trouble out here last night during the fire. You can lose a lot of points with your friends if you spy on them."

The clown stared hard at the girl. Amy gulped when she realized what Uncle Bunkie was saying. Somehow the funny clown seemed to know that Amy had been at the field when the fire had started. But how could he have known, Amy wondered?

"It's time you ran along, young lady," the clown said, folding his arms across his polka-dot chest. "We can't have children in the way."

"Ok," Amy said. She turned her bike toward town and began pedaling. She rode about fifty yards before looking back. The tall clown was still watching her, his arms folded across his chest. Amy got an uneasy feeling in her stomach. She pedaled the rest of the way into town and didn't look back.

Amy rode home. She ate lunch by herself since her stepmother was lying down to take a nap. Amy was glad to see her asleep since she didn't want to be told to study. She went up to her room and watched some television. At a quarter until three, she went outside and got her bike.

When she arrived at Bicycle Hills, it seemed like half the kids in town were there. Everyone had heard that something new and exciting and fun was happening out at Bicycle Hills, and they wanted to see what it was about. The mysterious dark wall was already up around Bicycle Hills. Each of the four sides was about as long as a football field. The wall was so high you could only see the tops of just a few hills inside. Amy parked her bike and ran over to the wall for a better look. The shiny dark walls were smooth and hard to the touch. When Amy saw her dark reflection looking back at her, she suddenly felt queasy. She shook off the feeling and stepped away from the wall.

The entrance into Bicycle Hills was near the corner of the field closest to the cemetery and the road. A crowd of children was gathered around the entrance, waiting to go inside. Amy wormed her way through the crowd for a better look. A little booth, like a ticket booth to a movie theater, had been attached to the wall. But the booth appeared to be empty. On the front of the booth was a black panel of plastic about two feet square. On the bottom was a thin slot two inches wide.

Amy was looking at the booth when a shout and a cheer went up in the crowd of children. Uncle Bunkie had suddenly appeared from inside Bicycle Hills. He was on the golden Super Wings bicycle, perched right on the top edge of the wall just above the ticket booth. Amy wondered how the clown could keep his balance since the bicycle tires were wider than the edge they were resting on. Yet the bicycle stayed steady.

"Hey, kids, are you ready for some fun?" Uncle Bunkie shouted.

"Yessssss!!!" the children shouted back.

"I'm glad to see all my little Centerville friends want to have fun, fun, fun in Bicycle Hills," Uncle Bunkie said in his bouncy voice. The children in the crowd clapped and cheered.

"When can we go inside?" a voice shouted out.

"All in due time," the clown said with a twinkle in his eye. "First things first. Let me tell you a little about our game. Caves and Cobras is a game of pretend, but it's more than pretend too. The first series of games will be finished by Halloween. The winners will receive a special prize—a Trag 7 power unit. As I demonstrated earlier this morning, the Trag 7 power unit will make your Super Wings bicycle do things no

57

ordinary bicycle will do. In fact, with a Trag 7 in place, you can do more things and go more places than you can dream or imagine. But in Bicycle Hills, anything is possible because it's the place of your dreams . . . or my name isn't Uncle Bunkie."

"How do we get those units?" Barry Smedlowe yelled.

"Like everything else in life, you need the points in the Point System to qualify," the clown replied. "It's performance that counts. Goliath Industries would like every child in this town to have a Trag 7, but first, they want to see if you are worthy to own one."

The children murmured, nodding their heads up and down.

"How do we prove we're worthy?" Sloan asked.

"By winning the game, of course," Uncle Bunkie said. "It's performance that counts . . . and wins."

"But how do we win?" Barry yelled out.

"For now, that's a secret, but you'll learn once you start to play," the clown said mysteriously.

The children in the crowd began talking excitedly among themselves. Though many of them hadn't seen Uncle Bunkie's demonstration of the mysterious Trag 7 that morning, they had heard about its wonders from their friends.

"You said you put those Trag 7's on a Super Wings bicycle," someone shouted out. "They'll work on other bicycles too, won't they?"

"I'm afraid not," Uncle Bunkie said. His big red nose drooped sympathetically when the children began to frown. "The Trag 7 is so special, it only works with one kind of bike, the Goliath Super Wings."

A groan went up in the crowd. The golden Goliath Super Wings bicycles were expensive. But does it have to be a Super Wings? They were also hard to find even if you could afford one.

"But most of us don't own Super Wings bicycles," Barry Smedlowe blurted out. "The stores never have them in stock."

"I own a Super Wings," Sloan Favor said so everyone could hear. "And everyone in my club owns one too."

The crowd murmured again. Sloan Favor and his club instantly gained several points.

"Well, I do have some additional good news," Uncle Bunkie said. "On Monday morning, a new shipment of Super Wings bikes will arrive at the toy store. As you all know, they cost a lot of money, but they are very special bikes. I understand that times are hard, so I am prepared to make a deal if you want a Super Wings. I can accept your old bicycle in trade as the down payment, and we can work out the details of how you can make the payments. If you are interested, come by the toy store on Monday after school. I will sell them on a Point System basis. The better your rank, the more likely you are to get a new bike."

The children began talking again. Amy looked around. Many of the kids seemed worried. Barry Smedlowe was arguing with one of his friends. Uncle Bunkie watched them with an amused grin on his face.

"Hey, kids! How many of you want to go inside Bicycle Hills right now?" the clown shouted.

A loud cheer filled the air as the children yelled and raised their hands. Amy's hand shot up in the air too.

"Unfortunately, Bicycle Hills can't take all the children in town at once," the clown said in his normal happy voice. "So we will use your number card rank. Line up at the entrance booth. When it's your turn, put your number card in the slot provided. The booth is connected to the Big Board in my store. If you qualify for today, your card will be returned with a small stamp on it that looks something like a bicycle wheel. If you receive an entrance mark, then bring your bicycle to the gate. Once you're inside Bicycle Hills, I'll tell you the rules of the games."

The children ran for the entrance booth all at once. Amy was near the front of the line. She pulled out the small dark card. On one side was the dark shadowy picture of Amy's face. On the other side it had the white rank number—seventy-eight. Amy waited patiently, wondering about the new game. Every one of the children in front of her qualified to get in Bicycle Hills. They would put their number card into the slot. The black screen would flash their name, number rank and sign of approval in bright purple letters.

Amy stepped up to the board with confidence. Being ranked number seventy-eight was an honor because she was in the top hundred. The best score to have was Number One, of course. The girl in front of Amy had been ranked one hundred forty-four, and she had been approved quickly. But when Amy stuck in her number card, the black screen seemed to take longer than usual. The black panel spit her card back out. Not only was she not approved to enter, but her number had been changed. Her new ranking had dropped all the way down to three hundred twelve. Amy stared at the number in disbelief.

"Hurry up," the boy next in line demanded. He pushed Amy out of the way so he could put his card in the slot.

Amy moved to the side, staring at the small number card. Beyond the tall dark walls she could hear the children playing inside Bicycle Hills. Though she couldn't see them, she knew they must be riding around the dirt track, shooting up and down the hills.

Amy looked back down at the card. She couldn't figure out why she didn't qualify to go inside with the others nor why her rank number had fallen so dramatically. She waited patiently until all the children had gone through the line and into Bicycle Hills. Four other children didn't qualify, so they rode back toward town. But Amy waited. Uncle Bunkie was standing by the gate. Amy rolled her bicycle over to him.

"There's been some kind of mistake," Amy said. "I was ranked at seventy-eight, and it went down to three hundred and twelve."

"There couldn't be a mistake," Uncle Bunkie said. "That screen is hooked up to the Big Board in the toy store. You have to be in the top three hundred to get inside today. Apparently, your rank dropped."

"But how can my rank have dropped so quickly and so low?" Amy asked. "I've never been below a hundred. There must be a mistake somewhere."

"The Big Board doesn't lie," the clown said with a smile. His nose glowed on and off once. "I suggest you come by the store on Monday and buy a Point Breakdown sheet. Then you can locate the problem in your score. Now if you'll excuse me, I need to tell the qualifying children the rules of the game."

Before Amy could protest, the clown closed the solid door. Amy stood outside the tall walls, holding onto her bicycle. She had never felt more left out in all her life, especially when she heard the crowd of children inside. Then she got on her bike. As she rode slowly back into town, angry tears came while the children cheered within the distant walls.

LEFT
OUT

· · · · · · · ·

6

The feeling of being left out stayed with Amy the rest of that weekend. Her sudden drop in the Point System was bad enough. But on both Saturday and Sunday night her parents went to the newly opened Goliath Country Club and left her with little Sarah Jane. She had baby-sat before with other people's children. But baby-sitting your own sister was harder. Amy had little patience with the baby's cries and messes. And having to do it two nights in a row seemed like double punishment.

She was glad when school came on Monday. But her feelings quickly changed when she got to her homeroom. Almost everyone was talking about Bicycle Hills, but in secretive ways. Amy tried to join in a couple of times, but the other children would suddenly get quiet. Amy tried to talk to Tiffany Favor about what had gone on in Bicycle Hills during lunch. But since Amy hadn't qualified to get inside the walls, Tiffany acted more distant than ever.

"I'd like to tell you since you're my neighbor," Tiffany said. "But Uncle Bunkie said it's against the rules to talk about the games to those who haven't been inside, or else we could lose points. All I can say is that it's the most fun I've had in a long time. And Uncle Bunkie says Bicycle Hills just gets better the longer you play there."

"I don't understand how I could drop rank so quickly," Amy said.

"You must have done something wrong somewhere to go all the way down to three hundred twelve," Tiffany replied. "I'd die of embarrassment if I fell that low. I rank number five right now."

Tiffany showed her number card to Amy and then walked away. Amy felt like all her classmates were acting cool toward her. And they seemed different in other ways too, though Amy couldn't quite put her finger on it. Then she decided they looked different. They looked slightly pale, as if they were recovering from some illness. Amy wondered if some kind of flu or cold bug was going around.

The only friendly face she saw that day belonged to John Kramar. He seemed glad to see her and smiled. But Amy didn't smile back. She treated him like Tiffany and the other girls treated her. She tried to act like she hadn't even noticed him. Ever since she had taken that wild ride that night on the Spirit Flyer bicycle, things had been different. They weren't differences you could explain very easily, but she felt different inside. She thought about seeing that place they called the kingdom and the one they called the Prince of Kings. Something about the Prince seemed very wonderful and appealing. Much of her longed to see him again and have the chance to talk to him. But every time she thought of him and the mysterious and glorious kingdom, her mind was flooded with thoughts about the creepy chain she had seen and the bad feelings it had caused. She still wondered why it had all happened. She had tried to push that whole situation with the Spirit Flyers out of her mind, but secretly she worried about that odd chain that seemed invisible and what it meant.

As the day dragged on, Amy felt more left out than ever. The more she wanted to be a part of her group of friends, the colder they acted.

After school let out, Amy went to the bicycle racks with the others. The girls talked excitedly about Super Wings bikes and Bicycle Hills. As Amy unlocked her bike, she heard Mary Jane talking in a smug whisper. ". . . half the kids in town got in, but not Amy. Even Dora Smuckler got in. If Amy's such a Miss Know-it-all, why can't she get in? Maybe she could use some Brownie points from the teacher to get her in. . . ."

The girls laughed as they rode off. Tears came to Amy's eyes. Then she got angry. She got on her bike and pedaled right for the toy store. She was determined to find out why her rank had dropped so low. Amy calmed down as she rode down the quiet streets. She pedaled down Tenth Street to the town square. Most of the stores in Centerville were located along the square or on North or South Main Street. Happy Toy Store was located on South Main Street in the first block below the square.

As she stopped for a red light, Amy noticed some men putting up a new sign on a billboard on top of the music store on the west side of the square. The sign was written in large black letters on a plain white background.

****

Get Centerville in ORDER!!!
Put Big Boards in City Hall.

****

Amy stared up at the man and woman putting up the sign. Though Amy had only been in town a couple of weeks, she knew that an election was coming up soon in November. And she also knew from hearing her father and mother talk that a new political party, called the ORDER party, had been organized in Centerville recently. Most of the people who belonged to this party worked out at the big Goliath Industries factory. Since he worked for Goliath, her father had been asked to help campaign. A lot of the meetings took place out at the Goliath Country Club.

Amy didn't know much about politics, but she did know about Big Boards and the Point System. Her sudden drop in score over the weekend seemed to put her whole future in question. But as Uncle Bunkie said, a Point Breakdown would point out the problem.

Amy rode down the sidewalk until she came to a stop underneath a purple sign that blinked on and off—*HAPPY TOY STORE*. Dozens of bicycles were parked by the front door. She was surprised there were so many until she remembered about the new shipment of Super Wings.

She got off her blue ten-speed bike, knocked down the kickstand and went inside. The store was packed with noisy children. Uncle Bunkie was standing by a row of shiny new Goliath Super Wings bicycles. Barry Smedlowe was waving his number card and talking. Amy ignored the commotion and walked over to the far wall of the toy store where there was a long black shiny panel, one of the Big Boards. The top of the Big Board was lit up in purple lights, spelling out the words:

*********************** THE POINT SYSTEM ***********************

Amy dug four quarters out of her front pocket. On the lower left corner of the mysterious dark panel was a coin slot, just like in a soda machine. Amy fed the dollar's worth of quarters into the Big Board. The dark panel made an electric humming noise once it received the coins. Amy inserted her number card. The small girl then stepped back and spoke, "Big Board, Big Board on the wall, give a Point Breakdown of my all in all."

The Big Board whirred into action as numbers and letters flashed across the surface of the darkness. Finally a bell rang as two pieces of computer paper rolled out of another slot right below the coin slot.

When the paper stopped moving, Amy ripped the sheets off. There was no mistake. She frowned as she read the news:

****

Amy Burke: Level: 1   Rank: 312   Score: 764

****

The rank number was in big black letters at the top of the first sheet. Amy sighed. The number was indeed official. She folded the paper and quickly walked outside. She was glad all the other kids were intent on making deals to get Super Wings bicycles. She still felt embarrassed to be so low. She had been hoping it had all been some kind of mistake.

Children were rushing from all directions to find out if they could qualify for a new Goliath Super Wings. Amy pushed her bike into the street and rode toward the town square. She pedaled across the street to the center of the square. She jumped her bike up on the sidewalk and coasted to the steps of the old gazebo. Amy got off her bike and sat down on the steps to read her scores.

Amy had seen Point Breakdown sheets before. A person had different categories which were arranged in alphabetical order. Each category was broken down into specific things in which a person received plus or minus points, which in turn gave the score for that category.

The all-important Appearance was the first category on the list. Amy looked through each item like height, weight, cuteness, hair, smile, skin tone and so forth. But her scores looked normal there. Then she went on through the other categories—Conformity Quotient, Family Status, Friends . . .

Amy looked again. There was a huge minus points score in the Friends category. "I've never gotten minus points there before," Amy said to herself. The Friends category was broken down into four areas:

(1.) Number of people who like you, (2.) Number of people who don't like you, (3.) Number of people who don't care, and lastly, (4.) Questionable acquaintances.

The scores all looked bad, but especially the last part on Questionable acquaintances. There in red letters and numbers were over four hundred minus points. The Point Breakdown told the reason.

****

Questionable Acquaintances: Subject in questionable contact
with several Rank Blank children who possess
Spirit Flyer bicycles. Subject gave permission for actual contact
with Spirit Flyer. Outcome uncertain. Remedy: Break all contacts.

****

Amy gulped and blinked. Then she saw more red markings in the next category below Friends. This category was called Future Potential. Amy was surprised again that she had negative points here too. After all, she had always been fairly popular, and she assumed that it would always be that way. She thought her future was secure since she did ok at school, looked nice and knew her parents could pay her way to college. But the Point Breakdown score glared in red minus points. As she looked through the specific items, it wasn't hard to find the problem. It was right at the very bottom of the category.

****

Future Potential: Questionable. See Friends: Questionable
acquaintances. All could be lost.

****

"All could be lost?" Amy asked herself out loud. "Just because that Kramar boy gave me a ride on his bicycle?" Just then, Amy heard voices. She looked up. Tiffany and a bunch of her friends from school were crossing the street. Amy quickly folded up the Point Breakdown sheet and stuck it in her pocket. She didn't want to compare scores. Everyone always wanted to see other people's Point Breakdowns.

"Hi, guys!" Amy said to the girls. They looked at her quietly. Tiffany stopped pedaling. Since Tiffany stopped, the other girls stopped too.

"We're going out to Bicycle Hills," Tiffany said. "Are you going to try to go inside?"

"Not today," Amy said miserably. "I'd come along, but I've got to catch up on some school work."

"Let's go!" a girl named Mary Ann said. "I want to be sure to get one of those Trag 7 boxes by Halloween. Miss Math-whiz has to do her schoolwork and can't play. Besides, she doesn't qualify to get inside anyway." The other girls laughed and started to pedal away.

Amy felt a ball of frustration rise up inside. Before she knew what she was doing, she yelled after them. "I'll have a Trag 7 before any of you guys," Amy called out. "In fact, I already might have one."

Tiffany pulled the hand brake on her bike. The other girls stopped. "What did you say?" Tiffany asked.

"I said I'll probably have a Trag 7 power box sooner than Halloween," Amy replied nervously.

"Sure she will," Mary Ann said. "Let's go."

Amy watched Mary Ann and the other girls pedal away. But when they got to the corner, Tiffany turned around. She talked with the other girls for a moment. Then they rode on, but Tiffany pedaled back to Amy.

"What did you mean about having a Trag 7?" Tiffany asked. "They all think you were making a joke or talking big."

"Well, I wasn't," Amy said angrily. She was still mad about feeling left out all day. "I have one of those boxes right in my house."

"You're kidding," Tiffany said. "Why haven't you used it?"

"Well, it's not mine, exactly," Amy said. "My father has it."

"That's right!" Tiffany said. A light lit up in the popular girl's eyes. "Your dad has a really good job in research and development. I bet he can get all kinds of stuff from Goliath."

"Your dad is the second most important man at the factory," Amy said. "Doesn't he bring home things?"

"Nothing like a Trag 7 unit," Tiffany said. "A lot of that stuff is secret. My dad manages the factory, but he doesn't bring stuff home. How did your dad get a Trag 7? Do you think we can borrow it?"

"I thought you were going out to Bicycle Hills," Amy said.

"That can wait," Tiffany said.

Suddenly, Amy realized she had gained entrance to the inner circle of girls and that felt good. She intended to enjoy every minute of it. As they rode toward home, Tiffany asked question after question. And she was still asking questions when they got to Amy's house.

THE
WARNING
· · · · · · · ·
7

Amy felt as if she were walking on a cloud
the next day at school. All the girls were acting friendly to her. Tiffany
asked Amy to sit with them at lunch. Amy knew that made her points
go back up because Tiffany considered her a friend. Of course, there
were a few dark sides to the cloud Amy was floating on. Tiffany had been
so interested in the Trag 7 box that Amy had gotten carried away in
talking about it. In fact, she had said things that weren't quite true. "I
didn't really lie," Amy told herself later. "I just let Tiffany draw her own
conclusions."

At home the box hadn't been in her father's study like Amy had hoped. But there was a photograph of it in some papers on top of his desk. "Let's just keep this a secret between us for now," Tiffany had said.

"Sure," Amy had agreed quickly, wondering if she had said too much to her popular neighbor. Amy had acted like she could get one of the mysterious Trag 7 boxes when she wasn't at all sure that was true. Her father had been secretive about the box the only time Amy had seen it. He hadn't acted like he wanted her to know much about it. But Amy pushed those thoughts out of her mind at the lunch table. All that mattered was that she was accepted by the most popular girls in her class.

"Why don't you check your score again today down at the Big Board," Tiffany asked as they were finishing up lunch. "I'm sure you must qualify to get in Bicycle Hills by now."

"I should hope so," Mary Ann said.

"Is Caves and Cobras a hard game to play?" Amy asked excitedly. She had heard many different things about the new game in the last few days, but only bits and pieces.

"Well, you're not supposed to tell," Tiffany said. "But it's kind of like being on a treasure hunt . . ."

"The treasure is hidden . . . and you try to find it," Mary Ann added. "It's the most fun. And you get to pretend you're different people . . . like warriors and fighters."

"And your powers and rank increase as your points increase," Tiffany said. "But we better stop talking. Just take our word for it. The games at Bicycle Hills are better than any I've ever played."

"Not to mention just riding up and down the hills," a girl named Heather said. "That's absolutely dreamy. Everything about Bicycle Hills is dreamy if you ask me. I wish I had a Rainbow Dream Drop right now."

The girls all looked at each other and giggled. Amy suddenly felt left out of their fun again. Their eyes looked wet and unfocused. Then Amy remembered how pale they looked. Tiffany and Mary Ann looked better than the others, but Amy could see they were wearing makeup.

"Well, I hope I can get in this time," Amy said, trying to ease her fears. "I'll check down at the Big Board in the toy store after school. I have a feeling my points have gone up."

The rest of the school day dragged by. Though she tried to think about her school work, Amy's mind kept wandering to Bicycle Hills. She wondered what it was really like inside the dark walls, and how the mysterious game was played. As soon as the bell rang, Amy bolted from the school. She hopped on her bike and headed for the toy store. Once there she didn't waste any time. She went straight to the Big Board, stuck in her number card and put money in the slot. "Big Board, Big Board, on the wall, how do I rank among them all?" The Big Board roared into life. Bells rang as lights flashed. Then the words stopped, frozen in the darkness:

****

Amy Burke: Level: 1   Rank: 33   Score: 970

****

"Wow! I'm in!" Amy shouted. "I knew my score couldn't be way down for long. Now it's even better." She pulled her number card out of the slot. Just like the Big Board had said, her new rank was right there on the card. Amy kissed the two threes and ran out of the store.

She zoomed down the streets heading for Cemetery Road. She could hardly wait to get to Bicycle Hills. Nothing else seemed to matter except getting inside those walls and having fun with her friends.

But then something happened. Just as she was turning on to Cemetery Road, she heard someone calling her name. Amy slowed down and looked behind her. But she didn't see anyone. She sped up, thinking she was just imagining something. Then she heard her name again. Only this time it was louder, as if it was right on top of her.

Amy looked all around her. But again she saw nothing. Then she looked up as she saw a motion. Amy gasped and squeezed the brake so hard she left a ten-foot skid mark. She hoped she was only imagining things as she saw John Kramar on his big red bicycle slowly floating down out of the sky right before her eyes. He landed softly on the pavement in front of her. At first Amy felt a sense of wonder shake inside her at the sight of the old bicycle. Then suddenly she just felt angry because of the fright he had caused.

"I didn't mean to scare you," John Kramar said, seeing her frown.

"Well, you did," Amy said. She stared at the mysterious old bicycle. "Why don't you just leave me alone?"

"But I had to come," John said. "The kings wanted me to come. The Spirit Flyer brought me here to warn you about Bicycle Hills."

"What do you mean?" Amy demanded, glaring at John. "I think you're crazy and so is that bike. I want you to just leave me alone." Amy started to pedal again. She just got past John when he spoke again.

"But I have to warn you," John said. "What they're playing is only a game for now, but soon it will be for keeps."

Amy was about to keep pedaling, but her curiosity made her stop. She whirled around and faced John. "What are you talking about?"

"I said that Bicycle Hills seems like fun now, but something else is going on," John said slowly. "Something deeper. We think it's just one of the plans Goliath Industries has to take over the town, to make everyone slaves to their chains forever."

At the mention of the word *chain,* Amy suddenly felt a heaviness come on her, like the night of the fire. She looked at the ground. Part of her was being pulled toward Bicycle Hills. But part of her wanted to remain with this strange boy and hear him out. She still wondered what she had seen that night of the fire.

"I told you I don't believe in any of that stuff," Amy said. "No one's a slave around here. There haven't been slaves since the Civil War."

"But you saw the kingdom and the chain," John replied. His eyes were kind. "Don't you remember? It was only a few nights ago. Only we never got a chance to explain." The boy smiled.

He seemed sincere, Amy thought. Then she was flooded with fear as she remembered the chain. "I don't know what I saw for sure," Amy said defensively.

"Don't you remember how the Spirit Flyer rescued you?" John asked. "And you saw the kingdom or at least a part of it. You can be free from the chain. And the kings will give you a Spirit Flyer too."

"Uncle Bunkie made his bike fly too," Amy said. "Lots of kids saw it. Last Saturday in Bicycle Hills. He was flying all over the place."

"Really?" John asked. Suddenly the boy looked troubled.

"That's right," Amy replied, seeing she had confused the boy. "He was flying around just like an airplane. All it takes is a Goliath Super Wings bike and Trag 7 power unit. And you don't have to worry about any of those stupid chains or weird stuff happening."

John was silent for a moment, thinking. He touched the handlebars of his old red bicycle carefully. As he did, Amy turned to ride away.

"Wait!" John called. He rode after Amy. She didn't stop pedaling so John rode beside her. "Even if he did all those things, it doesn't mean they're good," John said. "It sounds dangerous to me. If it comes from Goliath, something has to be wrong with it."

"Who says?" Amy demanded without slowing down. "Flying is flying. It doesn't matter what bike you're on or who made it."

"But of course it does. It all depends where the power comes from: whether it's from the Kingdom of the Kings or the domain of darkness."

Amy didn't say anything but kept pedaling. John looked frustrated and Amy felt pleased to see that he was confused for a change. They rode side by side down Cemetery Road. As they passed the factory, the boy spoke again. "I can show you the deeper difference if you give me a chance," John blurted out.

"Show me what difference?"

"The difference between the kingdom and the domain of darkness.

Maybe if you saw it, you would realize there's a kind of war going on."

"What war?" Amy asked. "You're kidding me again."

"There's a war going on in the Deeper World," John Kramar said. "And it affects people like you and me here in Centerville. That's what was happening the night of the fire."

"The only wars I've heard about are the ones I've seen on TV," Amy said. "But those are in faraway countries, not here."

"Those smaller wars are really just a part of the ongoing fight in the Deeper World," John said.

"I wouldn't call those wars so small," Amy said seriously. "My dad is worried that they might start using nuclear bombs and space weapons. It could turn into a terrible world war, he says. The biggest war of all."

"Well, the war in the Deeper World is already the biggest world war of all time in a way," John said. "Everyone in history has been affected by the war between the kingdom and the domain of darkness. It's a battle between what's really good and what's really evil."

"How do you know all this?" Amy asked.

"It's written in a book," the boy replied. "You can read about it yourself in *The Book of the Kings*. I could give you a copy and you would understand more about the kings and the kingdom and the chain."

Part of Amy wanted to dismiss the whole conversation with this persistent boy. Yet a part of her wondered what he was talking about. He did seem concerned about her.

"I can show you more if you let me," John said.

"Ok," Amy said. "Show me. Just don't aim that light at me like you did the other night."

"We need to take a ride together," John said.

"Ok," Amy said.

"I mean, on the Spirit Flyer," John said. "You can't see unless you get on a Spirit Flyer."

"Are you sure?" Amy asked. John nodded. Amy sighed. Then she pushed her bicycle into the cemetery and laid it down behind the first row of graves. Though she was suspicious, part of her wanted to trust John. After all, he had saved her the night of the fire, hadn't he? And he was quite a handsome boy, too, she thought.

John smiled as Amy climbed on the back of the Spirit Flyer. He pedaled slowly down Cemetery Road. Amy held onto his waist. Without warning, John seemed to bend the handlebars on the old red bicycle so they aimed toward the sky. The big front tire left the pavement first, followed by the rear. "Hold on!" John said.

"You didn't say you were going to do this," Amy cried. But as soon as she spoke, her fear was replaced by a sudden calmness. For some reason, riding on the big red bike made her feel safe because it seemed so stable, even if the wheels weren't touching the ground.

"I'll go slow," John said over his shoulder.

He turned the bike toward the cemetery. He flew slowly over the gate and the rows of graves, about five feet off the ground. He guided the bike through the trees and kept pedaling until he was at the back of the cemetery. He stopped the bike in the air, facing Bicycle Hills.

"Bicycle Hills isn't just a place to have fun," John said seriously. "My Uncle Bill is the sheriff here, and he said that field used to be called Potter's Field, owned by the Potter family, who also used to own the toy store. There are a lot of stories about that Potter's Field. A long time ago, someone was hanged there and people said other strange things have happened. Then it all burned. And now Goliath Industries owns the field and the toy store. Goliath has put up those walls. Who knows what they've got planned?" John pedaled the old red bicycle in the air.

"Where are you going?" Amy asked.

"You have to be careful how you approach this place," John said. "You can't just get over the walls anywhere. They've got a strong power."

"You mean you're going over the walls of Bicycle Hills on this?" Amy asked. "But you're not allowed. And neither am I. And if they see me on this bicycle, I could lose points again. The Point Breakdown sheet said that I lost . . ." She yelped when John suddenly aimed the bicycle higher and sped up. They were approaching Bicycle Hills rapidly. "I don't want to go over the walls," Amy cried out. "Make it stop!"

The old red bicycle suddenly began to shake and rock as it got closer to the wall. John tried to hold it steady, but the bike acted as if it were caught in an invisible whirlwind.

"The horn is blowing," John said loudly. "They must know we're here."

"What?" Amy yelled. She wondered what John meant. She hadn't heard any horn.

They were only twenty feet away from the black shiny wall when John turned the bike. As soon as he turned, the shaking and rocking stopped.

"They do know we're here," John said slowly, looking back over his shoulder at Bicycle Hills.

"Who knows what?" Amy asked. Suddenly she was afraid again.

John aimed the Spirit Flyer higher into the air, just above the treetops of the cemetery. From that angle they could see beyond the dark walls of Bicycle Hills. To Amy the place looked the same, except the dirt hills looked like they had been ridden over a lot more. The racetrack path was very clear. It was like a large circle with an X inside.

"I told you I don't want to go," Amy said.

"I know," John replied. "But at least look from here and you'll see. You can see the circled X without the light."

Without hesitating, John reached forward and flipped on the lever on the broken headlight. There was a flash and a rush of wind. Amy gasped as the bicycle shook. In an instant, the whole landscape changed. Everything seemed to be under a dark shadow. Amy blinked. "Look there," John said, pointing ahead.

A great tall tower of darkness rose right up before their eyes. The darkness quivered in front of them where Bicycle Hills had been. The black walls appeared as if they'd shot up a hundred feet into the air. And somehow, the dark walls seemed to be more than walls. They were so utterly dark, they seemed to be made of compressed shadows, hard as

bricks. And as Amy looked longer, there seemed to be something else in the walls. Something whirled and churned like smoke in the darkness before them. At the corners of the wall, two dark swaying shapes rose into the air. Amy gasped when she saw that the shapes were like ten-foot-tall snakes. Their eyes seemed to be glaring at the bicycle riders. Amy didn't know when she had seen such ugly, strange creatures. Looking into their eyes made her feel as if her stomach was filled with ice.

"We couldn't break through now," John said sadly. "The walls are up and they have guards."

"Turn it off!" Amy said, covering her eyes. "I don't want to see anymore."

"Ok," John said with a sigh. He began pedaling. Amy kept her eyes squeezed shut until she felt the bike tires touch down safely on the ground.

She was almost afraid to look. But when she opened her eyes, everything was back to normal. They were in front of the cemetery near her own bicycle. The shadows were gone and the walls of Bicycle Hills seemed the way they always had.

"I didn't mean to scare you," John said. "But in one way, you need to be scared. Like I said before, there's a war going on. We think Bicycle Hills is some kind of fortress or something. We don't know what it is. But we know those aren't ordinary walls. And you saw the guards. They're some kind of Daimone."

Amy hopped off the strange old red bicycle. She went through the gate of the cemetery and got her own bicycle. "I don't know what's going on," Amy said. "But I do know I don't want to go on any more bike rides with you. Every time I do I regret it. It seems like all you do is scare me."

Just then, Amy saw a group of children riding on bicycles. They were coming toward them. "It's Tiffany and the gang," Amy said. "I've got to go. See you later."

"Don't go in there," John warned. "I'm telling you there's danger."

"You just don't want anyone to have fun," Amy said. She looked at the dark walls and once again felt afraid. She wondered if John was right.

"But you can come with me," John said. "All the kids with Spirit Flyers are out at my parent's old farm, playing flight tag and all sorts of things. It's lots of fun. You'd be welcome to come. You could ride on my bike or Susan's. There's nothing like playing in the kingdom."

"You mean there are more of those bikes?" Amy asked in surprise.

"There's probably about fifteen kids out there today," John said with a smile. "Some are older and some are younger than us. We may even form some kind of club. We can fly and be there in less than a minute."

Amy wondered who the other kids were and what they were like. Then she heard Tiffany and the others calling her name.

"Well . . ." Amy said. She looked over at the other girls. "Maybe another time. I've got to go now." Amy smiled and tried to shake off her doubts as she rode toward her friends.

INSIDE
THE
FACTORY
· · · · · · · ·

8

Amy pedaled up to the group of her girlfriends. She held up her number card showing her new rank. The girls all congratulated her excitedly. Then they saw John Kramar. They became quiet as he rode by. John turned his bike toward town and began pedaling.

"What were you doing with him?" Tiffany whispered as John passed. "Isn't he one of those Rank Blank kids?"

"We were just talking," Amy said.

"You should be careful," Tiffany warned. "It can hurt your score on the Big Board if you're seen with the wrong people. Where I used to live, those pointless Rank Blank kids were the real losers. There were a bunch of them, but every one of them ended up Rank Blank. I had a friend who even became Rank Blank herself because she hung around them too much. It must have been awful for her. She didn't even show up on the Big Board. Can you imagine?"

"I can take care of myself," Amy said, trying to sound confident but not too defensive.

"I hope so," Tiffany said with a smile. "Race you."

The girls sprinted down Cemetery Road, laughing and yelling as they pedaled. But Amy couldn't join in the excitement. She rode after the others, her mind still racing with questions.

"What if John's right?" Amy asked herself. "How could the walls go up like that? And what were those ugly creatures? Was I seeing things? I wish I could talk to Dad. But he's so busy." Amy coasted to a stop in front of the entrance to Bicycle Hills. The other girls were lined up, using their number cards to make the door open. One by one they went in, pushing their bikes. Tiffany was the last one to go inside before Amy.

"I think I'll wait," Amy said suddenly.

"You mean you aren't going in?" Tiffany asked in surprise. "But you have a great rank now. You qualify."

"I know, but I have to do something first," Amy said defensively. "I want to go by the factory and see my dad. I need to ask him a few questions."

Tiffany looked puzzled but then smiled. "I know what you're going to do. You're going to look for a Trag 7 in his office."

"Sure, that's it," Amy said and tried to smile.

"Well, remember, we're friends," Tiffany said. "If you find the box, let me know right away."

As the door opened for Tiffany, Amy gasped. The inside of Bicycle Hills had changed so much since the last time she had seen it. The place seemed almost like a carnival of fun. Everywhere she looked there were smiling children shooting up and down the hills on their bicycles. Many of the bikes were the brand new golden Super Wings. But not only that, there were children walking around in costumes or uniforms. Some were holding things that looked like toy guns or weapons of some kind. They were smiling too. Amy tried to see every bit of the place as quickly as she could.

"Are you sure you don't want to go inside?" Tiffany asked. She opened the door wider so she could see the fun. All the children seemed to be smiling and laughing. Amy began to have doubts about her doubts. Maybe there wasn't anything wrong with Bicycle Hills at all, she thought.

"I just need to do some things first," Amy said. "But I'll be back."

"I got to go. They're waiting for me inside," Tiffany said. "We're going under today."

"Under what?" Amy asked. Tiffany smiled mysteriously.

"When you come and start to play the Caves and Cobras, you'll find out. By the way, you'll have to sneak onto the factory grounds, I bet. I heard my dad tell my mom that they're being more secretive than ever about this big project they're working on. I'll see you later." Tiffany stepped back inside. The door to Bicycle Hills closed.

Amy pedaled up and down Cemetery Road in front of Bicycle Hills thinking of all the things that had gone on the last few days. "I hope I can get inside. Secret projects or not, I have a right to see my own father." Amy pedaled slowly toward the entrance to the factory. "I've got to get in," she said to herself. "He's always so tired and busy at home, but he'll have to talk to me if I go to his office."

Two big tractor-trailer trucks rumbled down Cemetery Road and turned into the gate. The gate was open, but all cars and trucks had to stop by the little guardhouse to get permission to go in. As the trucks waited, Amy had a brilliant idea. She pedaled as fast as she could toward the gate.

While the two drivers were talking to the man inside the guardhouse, Amy rode on the opposite side of the trucks so the guard wouldn't see her. In a moment she was through the gate, pedaling toward the big buildings. She almost expected someone to blow a whistle or call her name, but nothing happened.

Amy had only been in the Goliath Industries factory once before, but she was sure she could find her father's office. The three really large buildings were the places where Goliath manufactured their secret products. Her father's office and lab were located in a smaller building connected to the big buildings.

Amy pedaled to that building. She parked her bicycle out of sight behind some barrels, then went in the door. There wasn't anyone at the front desk in the reception room, so Amy went through the door that led to the rest of the office. Her father's office was at the end of the hall. The place seemed strangely empty, so Amy just kept walking. Her father's office door was shut. A sign on the door said Dr. Richard Burke. Amy went in and shut the door.

"Dad?" Amy called out. No one answered. The only sound was a faint pounding noise in the distance. "I wonder where he is?" Amy asked herself. Then she thought about the Trag 7 power unit. "Even if I found it, I wouldn't know what to do with it." She felt more than a little sneaky as she looked carefully around the office, but she didn't see anything. Then she went over to his desk. The computer was turned off. A daily calendar book was open on her father's desk. It showed his schedule for the day. A note was paper-clipped to the page and said, "Meeting: four o'clock." Amy looked at her watch. It was four-fifteen.

"No wonder he's not around," Amy said out loud. She walked slowly around the office. Then she opened the door that led into the laboratory. Amy had been in some of her father's labs before, but never this lab. It seemed similar to the others, except for the birds. Near the far wall were several birdcages and in each cage, little brown sparrows flitted back and forth nervously. Amy stared at the birds in surprise.

"Dad never mentioned that he worked with birds," she said. Amy stuck her finger through the bars of a cage, but the birds moved away. Their dark little eyes looked like glass beads. They made a lot of noise, so she backed away to look at the rest of the lab.

There were large computers and other technical instruments along one wall. In the middle of the room were big heavy tables with more microscopes, test tubes and beakers sitting on top. Some of the tables had plastic coverings over them. A long row of cabinet doors lined another wall. Amy tried to turn the handle of the first door, but it was locked. So was the next door and the next. All the doors were locked except the last door. Amy opened it and looked inside. It was only a closet. Several of her father's white lab coats were hanging on hangers. There were some boxes on a shelf above the hangers. Amy thought of looking in them just because she was curious. That's when she heard talking in her father's office.

Out of instinct, she stepped into the closet and pulled the door so only a crack was left. She didn't think her father would mind her being there unannounced, but the other workers might not like it. But as she listened to the voices, Amy was surprised. She didn't hear her father's voice. She looked out through the crack. That's when two men came into the room. The first was easy to recognize since it was Uncle Bunkie all dressed up as a clown. The other person was a very old, dried-up stick of a man. His skin was wrinkled and his head was covered with wisps of white hairs. Amy had only seen him once before, but she knew his name was Cyrus Cutright. He was the president of the factory. Some people said he was the most important man in town.

"Will he be ready or won't he?" Uncle Bunkie the clown asked. His voice seemed unusually serious to Amy.

"Everything should be ready by Halloween," Mr. Cutright said in his door-hinge of a voice. "He's in a meeting now, or he could show you himself. I just came in here for the experimental unit he's been working on. It's in one of these closets."

Mr. Cutright walked slowly down the row of closet doors. His shoes squeaked louder and louder as he passed each door. Amy held her breath and leaned back among the lab coats. The steps came closer.

When she was sure she would be discovered, Mr. Cutright stopped. He pulled a bunch of jangling keys out of his pocket.

Amy's chest was pounding like a drum. She was sure the two men had to hear the pounding. But Mr. Cutright didn't seem to hear anything. He opened the door of the closet next to the one where she was hiding.

"Here it is," Mr. Cutright said. Uncle Bunkie the clown walked over and lifted a large aluminum trunk from the closet. He carried it over to a heavy table and set it down. They opened the lid toward Amy so she couldn't see what was inside. Uncle Bunkie looked and smiled his enormous red smile. Cyrus Cutright nodded and then closed the lid.

"Once this project is complete, we should all be doing well," Cyrus said. "We're on schedule. Though this factory is just a link in the chain, we'll do our part and deliver the pieces the company needs on time. We'll have our rewards too, once the target day has passed."

"I'll be glad to be doing something other than working with those bratty kids," Uncle Bunkie said. He pulled a pack of cigarettes out of his pocket and lit one.

"Don't worry, you'll be rewarded for your time," the old man said. "I've talked to the ORDER headquarters, and we'll still be in this town when they redraw the boundaries for the new sections."

"Maybe I'll be mayor," Uncle Bunkie said.

"Or the sheriff," Mr. Cutright added with a laugh.

"Speaking of the sheriff, I keep seeing those Kramar kids snooping around," Uncle Bunkie said.

"We'll take care of them, just like we do the rest of the children who don't cooperate," the factory president said. "There's getting to be too many of them for my comfort. That Bayley boy has become a real recruiter. His mother avoids me as much as possible. Her loyalties have slipped and after Halloween I've decided to take action on her."

"Well, I'll feel a lot better when this whole thing is over," Uncle Bunkie said. "I hope the bosses in Goliath and ORDER know what they're doing. I get a lot of calls and complaints about the Big Board in the toy store, especially from those Spirit Flyer parents. The complainers may be more organized than we imagine. I wonder if the election is as sure a thing as the Bureau thinks."

"Nothing will stop the ORDER to come," Mr. Cutright said. "Besides, the world will welcome a new ORDER. Your average citizen is tired of the depression and the threat of war. Over half the countries in the world are on the verge of economic collapse. That only adds to their fears. By the time the shift occurs, they'll be so afraid that they'll agree to any solution that gives peace and safety. After Halloween, they'll all get in line."

"I just hope things go as smoothly as you say," Uncle Bunkie replied. "What if the people don't like the changes?"

"Their lives will only be changed slightly, at least at first," Cyrus Cutright said. "And most fair-minded people won't mind when they consider the alternatives. There will be a mopping-up time to put things into ORDER, of course. That's why we need all the power and leverage we can get, to convince any reluctant citizens to cooperate with us. No sensible person will resist the Order of the Chain for long. The government won't tolerate any weak links. So you need to do a good job on those kids. Make 'em happy. Then they'll be right where we need them when the changes start on Halloween. Children can make good bargaining chips with a worried parent."

Uncle Bunkie laughed in agreement as he lifted the long aluminum trunk and carried it out the door. Cyrus Cutright followed, the keys jangling in his pocket.

When she heard the outer door to her father's office close, Amy finally let herself breathe more freely. She listened carefully, then let herself out of the closet. Though she didn't understand what Uncle Bunkie and Mr. Cutright had said exactly, she didn't like the sound of it. She figured it was part of the secret project Goliath was working on. And her father appeared to be working with those men on their "project," whatever it was.

She knew she wasn't supposed to overhear the men talking. Her father called that kind of secret listening eavesdropping, and forbade it.

"Why did I come here?" Amy asked herself. The talk about chains had made her remember the Deeper Chain that John Kramar had shown her with his bicycle. No matter how hard she tried, she couldn't push that image out of her mind. She thought about looking for the Trag 7 unit, but decided she didn't want to risk being there any longer. She ran from the lab into the office. She stuck her head out the doorway to the hall. She didn't see anyone, so she ran. She jerked open the door to the reception room and headed for the door.

"What are you doing here?" a woman behind a desk asked.

Amy stopped. The woman looked serious and almost angry. "I just came to see my dad, Dr. Burke," Amy said quickly. "But I'm going now. Bye."

Before the woman behind the desk could say anything, Amy went out the door. She hopped on her bike and stood up on her pedals. She headed straight for the entrance gate.

The phone rang inside Cyrus Cutright's office. He quickly picked up the phone.

"I'm supposed to be in a meeting," Mr. Cutright said harshly over the phone. Then he listened. "Who did you say just left?" He listened quietly. "How did she get in?" the old man asked. He frowned as he listened. "I see . . . Yes . . . No. I'll take care of it my own way. And I'll take care of you for letting in unauthorized people."

He slammed down the phone. He walked quickly over to his office window. He pulled aside the curtain and looked out. Down below, he watched a girl on a bike pedaling for the gate. He turned quickly and picked up a phone.

DR.
BURKE

· · · · · · · ·

9

Amy rode home, looking over her shoulder often. She parked her bike in the garage and went quietly inside her house. Up in her room, she finally stopped breathing so hard. She watched TV for awhile and then went downstairs to see about supper.

"Your father is going to be late again, so we might as well eat," Mrs. Burke said.

"I just hope he's not too late," Amy said.

"He can't be too late," her stepmother said. "We're going out to the club tonight."

"Again?" Amy whined. "It seems like he lives out at the factory or the country club."

"There's another important meeting," Mrs. Burke said. "Since your father works for Goliath, they expect him to do certain things. That's just politics."

"He never had to do this politics stuff in his old job," Amy said. "Maybe he shouldn't work for Goliath."

"Of course, he should," Mrs. Burke said. "They're the biggest company in the world. And they pay the biggest salaries too. I know you've been feeling neglected because of the baby and your dad's work, but things will get back in order soon."

"How soon?" Amy asked.

"Well, the elections come right after Halloween," her mother replied. "Things will settle down by then. Open that can of string beans and put it on the stove, please."

Amy helped her stepmother prepare the food and set the table. The meal seemed extra lonely to the girl without her father around. Amy didn't even feel hungry.

An hour later, just as she was taking the dishes out of the dishwasher, she heard the car in the driveway. Amy ran to the living room, but her stepmother had beat her to the door. Her father was already holding little Sarah Jane when Amy arrived. Amy waited for him to put Sarah Jane down and give her a hug, but he kept holding the baby as he walked through the house. Amy watched silently and then ran after him.

He was still holding the baby in the kitchen, bumping her up and down, saying funny goo-goo noises. Amy hated hearing her father talk that way. She thought it was silly and refused to talk that way herself.

"We left your place set at the table, Dad," Amy said. "I can put your plate in the microwave and warm it all up for you. We had meat loaf just the way you like it. I even helped some."

"Not tonight, Pumpkin," Dr. Burke said. "I had a quick bite at the factory cafeteria. Besides, I need to go over some data before we leave tonight. How did you do on that math test today?"

Just then the baby burped. Her father laughed and began talking to the baby again. He wasn't even waiting for Amy to answer. Amy felt like she would explode if she had to listen to another second of goo-goo talk. She walked quickly out of the kitchen and ran to her room. Amy flopped down on her bed, seething. For a moment, she wasn't sure if she hated her father or little Sarah Jane the most. She could see herself snatching little Sarah Jane out of her father's arms and throwing the baby across the room. Or she could see herself just grabbing her father by both ears and making him look into her face and talk to her. Of course, she knew she would never really do any of those things.

"Why bother?" Amy asked herself bitterly. She felt like crying, but she wouldn't give any of them the satisfaction of knowing how bad she felt. Amy lay on her bed thinking. Her stepmother called her. After Amy listened to a long list of instructions about what to feed little Sarah and so on, she ran up the stairs to her father's study.

She found him sitting at his desk. He was putting papers in a briefcase. Amy walked into the room slowly. "Do you guys have to go out tonight?" she asked.

"I'm afraid we do. It's an important meeting at the club."

"Meetings and work," Amy said with disgust. "That's all you do anymore. We haven't gone on a nature walk in weeks."

"I know that, Honey, but I've had a lot of deadlines to meet." Dr. Burke ran his hand through his hair. He looked tired, as usual. "It won't always be like this."

"But what are you working on? Why are they in such a rush?"

"The projects concern the government and they want them kept secret," Dr. Burke said. "I'm not supposed to tell anyone."

"Not even your family?"

"Nope, not even you guys."

"I think that's a rotten idea," Amy said. She pushed her way onto her father's lap. "Why are they so secretive? Everything about this town is secretive. Even the kids are keeping secrets."

"People are more on edge these days because of the depression," her father replied. "Too many people are out of work. Everyone is scared it might get worse, that the government is too unstable. And there was more bad news last night."

"What happened?" Amy asked.

"There was another attack overseas," her father said. "More bombs were set off in some oil tankers and in several oil fields. The war over there is just getting worse. Everyone is afraid our country will be drawn into it. There have been riots and protests in cities all over the world. Several South American countries are on the verge of revolutions. And to make things worse, some other countries have successfully launched new satellite weapons into space. No one knows for sure what's flying around up there."

"We won't really get into a big war, will we?" Amy asked.

"I don't know," her father said. He stared out across the room. "But I do know this: a lot of people in the government and Goliath are trying to prevent that from happening. I hope we succeed."

"Is that what Goliath is trying to do by Halloween?" Amy asked. "Trying to prevent a big war?"

Her father jerked so suddenly that Amy slid right off his lap and sat down hard on her bottom.

"What did you say?" he asked. He stared at her carefully.

"I said Goliath wants to change things by Halloween. So there will be order in the world, right?"

Her father stared at her quietly. He put his hand up to his mouth. "Where did you hear that?" he asked. Amy could tell he was acting differently. Something had changed, like a switch inside him.

"Just around," Amy said.

"You were at my office today, weren't you?" her father said. "I didn't believe them when they told me. Why were you there?"

"I went because I needed to ask you some questions," Amy blurted out. "Some odd things have been happening in this town. And I've heard some bad things about Goliath. Maybe you shouldn't work for them, Daddy."

"Why do you say that?" her father asked. "And what odd things have been happening?"

Amy was about to answer when she saw it. The black box that resembled the Trag 7 unit was on his desk under some papers. She lifted off the paper. She stared down at the box. The shiny surface reflected back a dark image of the girl's face, but there seemed to be something on her neck. She was about to pick up the box when her father grabbed her hand.

"What's wrong?" Amy asked in surprise. "What is that thing?"

"It's nothing you need to worry about," her father said quickly.

Amy looked at the small cube. He put the black box in an aluminum suitcase. There was foam padding with a square-shaped hole that seemed especially made to hold it. He snapped the case shut and locked it.

"What is that box?" Amy asked, looking at the locked case.

"It's technical," her father said.

"You always say that when you don't want to answer my questions," Amy said defiantly.

"Well, in this case, your question is hard to answer," her father said. "That little box is top secret. It's one of Goliath's products that I've been doing some experiments with as part of a larger project."

"Does that box do . . . strange things?" Amy asked. "I mean, does it have strange powers or something?"

Her father stared at Amy again quietly. He seemed surprised.

"You didn't play with one of these in my office, did you?" he asked.

"No," Amy said.

"Good," he replied, and seemed relieved. "Some of Goliath's best scientists invented this material and these boxes. I never met them because the whole team was killed in a fire of some sort, they said. A lot of their research was destroyed in the fire too. No one knows quite how these boxes work. Goliath has been having different scientists run experiments separately this time. I've been trying to figure it out and make applications. We work in separate labs in different places, but we pool our research."

"Any luck so far?" Amy asked.

"Well, frankly, I've been baffled by the whole thing," her father said. "I've never seen anything like it. It's almost like science fiction. There's a kind of energy or something that comes from the box, it seems. But it's very unstable. Even the plastic-type material it's made of is unstable. You analyze it one time and it appears to be one thing. Then run the same tests again under identical conditions and the results come out different. In my opinion, the box and the material have a lot of dangerous properties. But how could you have known about the energy field? This whole project is top secret. You're sure you weren't snooping around my office?"

"Not really," Amy said. "I was too busy hiding."

"Hiding? What do you mean?"

Then Amy told him the story about hiding in the closet. The more she said, the more surprised and troubled her father looked. When she finished talking, he was quiet for over a minute.

"First of all, I'm surprised at you for eavesdropping like that," Dr. Burke said. "And secondly, you're only a child. You can't jump to conclusions about things you don't understand. And finally, I want you to forget what you heard and never tell anyone. Do you understand?"

"But what did they mean about a new order coming?" Amy asked. "Are they going to take over the town? Some people say that right now. They say Goliath has bought up the bank and a lot of stores."

"Listen. This was a dying town until Goliath came here and gave people good jobs," her father said. A line of sweat was on his lip. "They are good for this town, not bad. Whoever says any different is mistaken."

"But is Goliath taking over stuff?" Amy asked. "I know they support that new party, ORDER. I've seen the signs in town. I bet that's what those meetings at the country club are about, aren't they? You're a member of that ORDER group."

"Jane and I are members of ORDER," her father admitted.

"Do you have to be members because you work for Goliath?" Amy asked.

"It's not only that," her father replied. He seemed irritable. "They have a lot of good, progressive ideas. We support what Goliath wants to do, not only here, but all over the world."

"But what do they want to do?"

"They want to prevent a terrible war from happening, first of all," her father said. "And that means new, somewhat drastic measures need to be taken. They don't see it as our country against another country. Borders just divide people. They want all the countries united, like one big happy family. They just want what's good for everyone."

"But how do you know what's good and what's bad?" Amy asked.

"I haven't got time to go into all this," her father said, looking at his watch. Amy was surprised to see his arm shaking.

"You almost seem afraid or something," Amy said. She looked at her father. "Do you think it's possible to be a slave and not know it?"

"What do you mean?" he asked while putting papers in a drawer.

"I was just thinking," Amy said. "Have you ever heard of the Deeper World? Or about a war going on in the Deeper World?"

"I don't think so," her father said, but Amy could tell he wasn't listening.

"Why do you have all those birds in your office?" Amy said. "Are they part of some experiment?"

"You didn't overhear Mr. Cutright say anything about the birds, did you?" her father asked with a frown.

"No," Amy replied.

"Good," her father said. He seemed relieved. "Jane and I need to get out to the club. Just don't worry about anything you heard or saw today, ok? Things will work out. Goliath will see to that. And that reminds me. Mr. Cutright gave me something special for you. I almost forgot."

Her father led Amy out of his study and down the stairs. She followed him out to the car. He lifted up the rear door of the station wagon and carefully pulled out a bicycle. Amy blinked in surprise.

"It's a Goliath Super Wings," she said.

"Top of the line," Dr. Burke said with a smile. "See, I told you not to worry. Goliath is looking out for all of us. Mr. Cutright said it was a bonus for me. He knows I've been working hard and that it's been hard on my family. He told me to give it to you especially. Do you like it?"

"Sure, I guess," Amy said. "They're the most popular bikes at school."

"They're popular all over the world. Now I hope you're happy. Just take the bike and have fun. Don't worry yourself about all this other stuff."

Just then, Mrs. Burke walked outside. She was dressed up and looked nice. "I left a list on the table for some last-minute instructions about Sarah," her stepmother said. "Be good."

Her parents got in the car. As they drove off, Amy stood in the drive-way holding the bicycle. Then she pushed it into the garage.

THROUGH
THE
WINDOW
· · · · · · · ·

10

Amy woke up the next day, irritable and confused. She had slept very little the night before. Her parents hadn't come home until late, and the baby had been fussy most of the evening, crying and unhappy. When her parents did finally get home, they had made so much noise that it woke Amy up. Her father had tripped on the stairs and fallen down. Amy had been worried and had gotten up. She had been surprised to find her father sitting in the hall, with an odd smile on his face.

Amy had smelled a chemical smell. Then she had realized that her father had been drinking some kind of alcohol. Seeing her father act so strange and foolish scared her. She hadn't gone to sleep for a long time, but drifted in and out of terrible dreams all night.

That morning at the breakfast table, her father was very quiet and looked pale and sickly, Amy thought.

"I'm sorry if I woke you up last night," her father said. "I got a little carried away out at the club. We were having fun and . . ."

"Were you drunk?" Amy stared at him in an accusing way.

"Your father was just tired and relaxed," her stepmother said. "With all these deadlines and the baby, we've all been under a lot of stress."

"We used to have fun on our nature walks," Amy said. "At least I did."

"And we'll have fun again," her father said. "I've got to get to work. I'm late. I'll see you all later. Maybe you can ride your new bike to school today, Amy. I hope you like it." Her father left. The baby cried and her stepmother left the table too. Amy ate only half a bowl of cereal when she decided she wasn't hungry.

"What's the use?" Amy asked herself and sighed. She took her cereal over to the sink, poured it down the garbage disposal and headed out for school. As she rode her Super Wings down the driveway she saw Tiffany. Her neighbor rolled up on her own Super Wings. When Tiffany saw Amy's new bike, she burst out, "You got one too!"

"My dad brought it home last night," Amy said flatly.

"That's great! You know, we've been wondering if you'd like to be in our Super Wings Club. Since more kids have been getting Super Wings, we thought of making the club larger. I'm sure you're club material." Tiffany and Amy rode to school together, talking about the club and rules. But most of all they talked about Bicycle Hills. "The best part about being in the club, is that we'll be winners of the C & C game for sure," Tiffany said. "And on Halloween, we'll each get a Trag 7 power unit for our very own. I can hardly wait to take off with the power of those things. Who knows what will happen?"

"How can you be sure the Super Wings will win?" Amy asked.

"We've been points ahead from the start. The only ones close are

Barry Smedlowe and the Cobra Club, but half of them don't even own a Super Wings yet. Plus we've been beating them at the game."

"How do you beat them?" Amy asked curiously.

"You'll see soon enough," Tiffany replied with a smile.

During the morning classes, Tiffany told everyone that Amy had a new Super Wings. All the kids seemed impressed. At lunch time, Amy sat with Tiffany and the other girls. Most of the kids were talking about Bicycle Hills when Amy sat down with her tray of food. Amy couldn't help but notice that most of the girls were wearing makeup that seemed almost too heavy. Their cheeks seemed too red. Mary Ann almost looked like a clown, Amy thought, but she didn't say anything.

"I'm going to be the first one through the window today," Mary Ann said.

"I'll be under before you," a girl named Marcia replied and laughed. "And down the elevator too."

"What window do you go through?" Amy asked.

"I'm not sure we're supposed to tell," Marcia said. "Are you going inside today?"

"Sure," Amy said. "Why not? I want to have fun like everyone else."

"Then you'll find out about the window soon enough," Tiffany said. She put her finger up to her lips. "Sssshhh! Here comes Mr. Compton."

Mr. Compton, the lunch monitor, walked slowly up and down the rows of tables. He leaned against the wall near Tiffany's table. Amy wanted to ask more questions but could see they wanted to keep it quiet.

The kids in the Super Wings Club met by the bicycle racks after school. Tiffany told Sloan about Amy's new bicycle.

"So you're finally moving up in the world, eh, Burke?" Sloan said. He smiled his perfect smile, his white teeth gleaming. A lot of girls thought Sloan was the definition of a cute guy. Amy hadn't thought much about it until that moment. His blond hair never looked out of place, even when he played sports. She wondered what Sloan thought about her.

She touched her curly hair with her hand, hoping it looked ok.

"Don't you think Amy should be in our club?" Tiffany asked.

"Sure," Sloan said. He smiled again. "How about it? Want to join the Super Wings? We've got the top-ranked kids in town."

"I'd like to be in the club," Amy said, staring up into Sloan's blue eyes.

"Good," Sloan said as he hopped on his bike. A bunch of guys were waiting for him at the other end of the bicycle racks. Every one of them was sitting on a golden Super Wings bike. "We're all going out to Bicycle Hills. Don't be too long. I think we'll be going through the window too. I've got some good battle plans for today."

The boys rode off. Tiffany and the other girls talked excitedly about Bicycle Hills.

"I've got to go home first," Amy said. "I need to ask my mom if I can go. I'll meet you out there."

"You have to ask your mom about something simple like that?" Tiffany asked. She seemed surprised.

"Well, that's not the only reason I'm going home," Amy said quickly. "I want to drop off my books too."

Amy pedaled home slowly. Carrying so many books under her arm wasn't easy. When she got home, she threw the books down on her bed. She told her stepmother she was going to Bicycle Hills and ran back outside before she could ask any questions.

The Goliath Super Wings could really whizz along once you got in high gear, Amy noticed. She figured it was the super lightweight frame that helped. It was easy to tell the difference between that bike and her old one. She headed north down Oak Street. She felt in her pocket to make sure she had her number card. That's when she saw them. There were ten, maybe fifteen big red bicycles parked out on the sidewalk. John and Susan Kramar were standing under a tree in someone's front yard.

"Hey, Amy!" John yelled. Amy didn't know what to do. He was smiling and seemed so hopeful. Amy smiled back. Before she knew it, Amy squeezed the brake on her Goliath Super Wings.

"Hi," Amy said as she coasted to a stop. She looked at John and Susan who were in turn staring at her Super Wings bicycle. Just then, Daniel Bayley ran out of the front door of the house.

"The other kids are about ready to go out to the farm," Daniel said. "We're going to have more fun than a barrel full of . . ." Daniel stopped and stared at the Super Wings silently. He looked up at Amy.

"I didn't know you had one of those bikes," John said.

"I just got it," Amy said. "My dad brought it home from the factory last night."

"I'm not surprised," Daniel said simply. "It's a kind of bribe. They do that when they get worried."

Amy was surprised at his words, though he hadn't said them in a mean way. She stared at Daniel with an open mouth.

"It was a bonus," Amy said defensively. "My dad's been working real hard, and they gave it to him for me."

"Whatever you say," the redheaded boy replied. "But my mom works there, and they gave her all kinds of stuff to give to me. Especially once I got my Spirit Flyer. And when I stopped riding the Super Wings over a month ago, they got really upset. They call them bonuses and gifts, but they're just bribes if you look at it in a deeper way. They bribe everyone first, but if that doesn't work, they threaten them. My mom has heard rumors that she's going to be fired after Halloween. Goliath is full of jerks."

"How can you say that?" Amy said. She felt herself getting angry. "My dad says Goliath is the best company around. He says they're doing a lot of good for this town and the whole world. All they want is peace for everyone."

"Well, we're not so sure what Goliath wants," John said. "But kids in town are changing, at least the ones that play at Bicycle Hills."

"What do you mean?" Amy asked.

"Well, a lot of kids are getting sick," Susan said.

"Kids always get sick," Amy said. "It comes with cold weather."

"Well, the school nurse told my dad that more kids are absent from school than usual," Susan replied. "Besides that, they have weird symptoms. They have lower than average temperatures. The nurse says it's in schools all over the state. They're worried it might be some new disease."

"None of my friends are really sick," Amy said. "Some of them are a little pale, maybe, but they don't complain."

"A lot of girls are wearing real heavy makeup, I've noticed," Susan said.

"There's nothing wrong with that," Amy replied.

"But that's not all," Daniel said. "We've looked at some of these kids with our Spirit Flyer Vision goggles, and they've changed in a deeper way."

"Yeah," John added. "It's like they have these shadows on them, shaped like snake scales."

"It reminds me of some kind of fungus," Susan said, making a face. "I know it must be connected to the sicknesses the nurse was talking about."

"And we think it's all connected to what's going on out at Bicycle Hills," Daniel added.

"How can you say that?" Amy asked. "Everyone I know loves it out there. In fact, I'm going out there, but I'm going to have fun."

"But don't you see the danger?" John asked. "You saw how those dark walls went up. That place is a regular fortress."

"All my friends have been playing out there for days and they enjoy it," Amy replied. "I don't think there's anything to worry about." And with that, Amy pushed off and headed down the road. John ran for his bike and hopped on.

"Let her go," Susan said, watching Amy pedal away.

"But she could be in danger," John said, looking after her.

"I think Susan's right," Daniel said. "She'll have to see for herself. And you can't blame her for sticking up for her dad. But maybe we can help her in some other way. Let's talk about it at the farm."

Amy was surprised to see a change when she got to Bicycle Hills. The tall wall around the field had been painted into a rainbow of colors. She pedaled over to the ticket booth. When she put the card in the slot, there was a humming noise and then the card came back out. "I'm in!" Amy said with pleasure. She pushed her bike forward. The door opened before she touched it. Amy hesitated for an instant and then rolled her Super Wings inside Bicycle Hills.

The whole place seemed strangely silent, Amy thought. Off in the distance, a couple of boys were zipping up and down some hills. A small building that looked like a concession stand stood near the wall by the road. A whole herd of bicycles were parked next to this building. Amy looked around once more. The insides of the walls to Bicycle Hills were unpainted. The black shiny material gave Amy a creepy feeling for a second, but she shook that out of her mind.

Amy got on her bike and rode slowly over to the well-worn dirt track. She pedaled hard to get up the first hill. Then she took off. She rolled down it like she was on a roller coaster and shot up the next hill. Amy rode to the far end of the field where the two boys were practicing jumps on a small hill off the main track. "Where are the other kids?" Amy asked. She recognized the older boys from school, but she didn't know their names.

"They went through the window," one boy said.

"The window?" Amy asked.

"Yeah, they went under for the C & C game," the other boy replied.

"I'm sort of new here," Amy said. "Where is the window?"

"In the big hill in the center, Stupid," the first boy said. The other boy laughed. Then they both pedaled back over to the main track and took off fast as they could go.

Amy sighed and then slowly pedaled over to a diagonal track that cut right across the top of the center hill. When she got closer, she noticed all kinds of bicycle tracks around the center hill. Amy rode around the bottom of the hill slowly, looking for a window. "I wonder what they were talking about," she said to herself. She suddenly felt hungry. She took a Rainbow Dream Drop out of her pocket, unwrapped it and popped it into her mouth. She got off her bike and ran up the side of the hill to the top. She didn't see anything unusual. But then she thought she heard screams and laughter somewhere off in the distance. Amy looked all around. She ran back down the hill by her bike. She cocked her head and listened. She heard voices that seemed far away.

Amy kept listening. She walked around the hill and the voices seemed to get louder. She kept walking and walking, listening at each step. Suddenly she was sure she heard someone calling her name. She thought she saw someone out of the corner of her eye, right behind her. She quickly turned and almost screamed.

Amy was looking back at a reflection of herself. She blinked her eyes and looked again. Right there, stuck in the side of the big hill, was a tall rectangle about three feet wide and six feet tall. The rectangle seemed to be made of shiny black plastic or glass, just like the walls around Bicycle Hills. A thin casing was around the outside edge of the rectangle that looked like a window or door.

"Where did this come from?" Amy asked herself. That's when she heard voices. And not only that, the voices seemed to be coming from beyond the window.

Amy leaned toward the darkness. For an instant, she thought she saw something else in the window, something moving far away. She moved closer. The voices were louder. Then she thought she saw a hand in the window. Amy wondered if it was a reflection of her own hand. She moved her hand but the hand in the window didn't move.

"Who's hand is it?" Amy asked out loud. She slowly reached toward the dark window. She felt both excited and afraid. Amy was almost touching the window with her own hand when it happened. The hand in the window suddenly reached right through the darkness like it was water or oil and grabbed Amy's wrist. She screamed and jerked backward, off balance. That's when the hand in the window yanked her forward. Amy screamed again and she fell headlong right into the dark window.

She heard a crash and a splash as she was sucked all the way through. The surface of the window quivered like the water on the top of a deep pond, then it was still.

THE
COBRAMAZE
. . . .
11

Amy was still screaming when someone put a hand over her mouth. She shook her head violently when she saw she was standing in a group of girls from school. Tiffany's hand was over Amy's mouth.

"Calm down, Amy," Tiffany said with a smile. "You act like a ghost has a hold of you. It's only me. I brought you in."

Amy looked around the group with wide eyes. There were eight girls, and each one was wearing a strange gray uniform or costume. But it was a uniform unlike any Amy had ever seen before. Each girl was also carrying a toy gun. The odd-looking clothes reminded her of some costumes she'd seen once in a science-fiction movie. What caught her eye first were the odd belts. Each one wore a belt that looked like a chain. And each round buckle had a metal circle with an X inside. Amy stared at the circled X.

The girls also had black gloves and wore a kind of hood. Right above their eyebrows the head of a cobra snake was printed on the hood. The back of the hood had snake scales that went down to their shoulders.

"Aren't these great costumes?" Mary Ann asked. The other girls looked at Amy with a smile.

"They're uniforms, not costumes," Tiffany said, correcting her. "These are Caves and Cobras commando uniforms. You wear them to play the game. They fit right over your regular clothes and zip up the front. And they have a built-in backpack to keep Glitter Pops and other things you need to play the game."

"They're like a coverall or a jump suit," Amy said.

"This shows your rank," Tiffany said, pointing to her left shoulder. There was a white patch with black embroidered thread that looked like links of chain. "We all start out as commandos at Link One. One chain or stripe signifies Link One. But you can go higher when you earn more points and experience in playing the game. You can have two chains, then three chains. As you gain points and tokens and experience you can advance to the War-link level, then War-lock. You can go all the way up to Cobramaster if you're really good. When you get to that level, you get a special colored Cobrahood. But we'll talk about that as we play. Come on."

"Where are we?" Amy asked as she looked around. They seemed to be in a small dome-shaped room that looked like the inside of a cave. Yet plenty of light came in the black window that she had been pulled through. The window wasn't nearly as dark from inside the hill. She could see outside as if she was looking through sunglasses. A bluish glow was also coming from the opposite end of the room.

"You're under the big hill in the center of Bicycle Hills," Tiffany said.

"But you haven't seen anything yet," Mary Ann added. The other girls nodded and smiled. "Wait until you see the Cobramaze. And we've only been playing on the first level. Uncle Bunkie hasn't opened the other levels yet. He says we're not ready."

"We've already started a game of Caves and Cobras," Tiffany said. "But since we knew you'd be late, we came back to look for you. Now you can play along with us."

Amy nodded. Something about the room seemed unreal to the girl. Maybe it was just the bluish glow and shadows that made it seem like a place in a dream. She was naturally drawn toward the glowing light at the far end of the room. As she walked toward it slowly, she saw it was a set of doors. Only these doors seemed to be filled with light or energy that made them glow. Whispers of an eerie blue smoke floated out through the edges of the frame. Next to the doors was a round object, about three feet high, that was made of stone and looked like a birdbath. A curved stone dish was on top of a stone pedestal. A blue flame erupted from a tiny hole near the rim of the dish. Amy figured it must be some kind of gas burner. A long shiny needle with a fine mesh chain attached to one end was lying near the flame. A small dark hole about three inches in diameter was in the center of the dish. Looking at the needle glistening in the blue light gave Amy the creeps.

"What's that for?" Amy asked.

"That's to open the door," Tiffany said. "This is your first time. You've got to give a drop for it to open."

"Give a drop?" Amy asked.

"Of blood," Mary Ann said.

"What?" Amy asked as Tiffany took her hand.

"It's only a drop," Tiffany said. She took the shiny needle on top of the plate and stuck it into the blue flame. "The needle is sterilized so it's safe. It's no worse than what the school nurse does for tests."

"But I don't know if I want to . . . ouch!" Amy yelped as Tiffany pulled the needle away. A tiny ball of blood appeared on the end of her right index finger. She stared at the blood in surprise.

"Hold it over the hole in the center and let it drip once," Tiffany instructed as she took Amy's hand. "Now squeeze it out."

Amy did so and the blood fell down the hole. Immediately the blue doors opened with a humming sound. Amy could tell it was an elevator, but not like any elevator she had ever seen before. The inside walls and ceiling were painted in bright rainbow stripes that blurred together.

"This is the rainbow elevator," Tiffany said. "They say it takes you beyond the rainbow to the land of your dreams, the Cobramaze." The other children walked eagerly inside. Amy followed. The big doors closed. Amy put the candy in her mouth as the elevator began to go down. Though it was hard to tell how fast they dropped, the elevator seemed to take a long time, and Amy began to feel slightly queasy as she stared at the blurry colors. Just then the doors opened.

"Let's go," Tiffany said. The girls ran through the doorway. Tiffany pulled Amy along by the hand, taking her into the first level of Bicycle Hills. The big blue doors swished shut behind them as soon as they were past them. Amy turned around quickly. The doors didn't have knobs or handles. Being beyond the doors gave her an odd sensation. She knew she had never been in a place like this before. The children were in a narrow hall about three feet wide that sloped down steeply about ten feet where it turned off to the right.

"Before we go any further, you need to take a Dream Drop," Tiffany said. "That's the good part."

"That's right," Mary Ann added. "It's part of the rules. A drop of blood, then a Dream Drop. They make everything seem dreamy and fun. Somehow they taste better once you take the trip down the elevator."

"Everything's better under Bicycle Hills," Diane said. She giggled, and so did the other girls as if they knew a joke that was a secret to Amy.

Tiffany had a small fat leather bag attached to her belt. She dug in and pulled out a handful of the rainbow-colored candies. Everyone watched as Amy popped one in her mouth. Then they all took one. Amy sucked on the candy. It did taste stronger. The mint was mintier and the fruits were juicier. But the medicine taste was horrible. For an instant, Amy felt dizzy and nauseous. Then it passed, and the rainbow-colored candy tasted delightful once more.

"We need to get back in the game," Tiffany said. "And you need a uniform. Normally you get them outside at the concession stand. But since we knew you were coming, we brought one for you."

"Just put it on over your clothes," Mary Ann said, tossing her a gray uniform.

Amy quickly pulled it on over her clothes and zipped it up the front. The uniform was made of some smooth synthetic material. She stepped into the legs and then put her arms through. She had a patch showing one link on her right arm. The left arm had a golden patch that said Super Wings. The same Super Wings insignia was on a patch about the size of a dinner plate on the front and back of the C & C commando uniform. A long zipper on the front closed it up. The metal of the chain belt was lightweight, like some kind of alloy. She fastened the chain with the odd circled X buckle. Then she pulled on the strange snakelike headpiece. The hood seemed a little snug and clammy, but the feeling passed. As she looked down at herself, she rather liked what she saw. She felt like she was ready for anything. The uniform didn't seem hot or uncomfortable. After she slipped on the soft black gloves, they gave her a toylike rifle.

"I got you a regular Faster Blaster," Diane said. "It's loaded with twenty Glitter Pop pellets. Don't waste them. You never know when you'll need them, and I didn't get you any refills. You can get other types of ammo too, like Fang Darts and Grenade arrows. But you have to earn more points in the game before you qualify for those."

"What will I need this for?" Amy asked, looking down at the strange toy weapon. But the other girls were already walking down the ramp and around the corner. She ran to catch up with them. When she rounded the corner, Amy blinked in surprise. The hallway had opened into a huge cavernous room about forty feet in diameter. Two big white zeros were painted on the wall. A small pool of green water with misty fog rising off the top bubbled up and fell down a smooth waterfall, making a stream which disappeared into a dark tunnel at the far end of the room.

Everywhere you looked, there appeared to be passageways and dark holes in the walls. There must have been over fifteen tunnels in the stone, and each one begged to be explored. Seeing the room made the girl's imagination run wild. She sucked hard on the candy in her mouth, wishing she had another piece.

"What is this place?" Amy asked. The other girls smiled.

"This is where the Cobramaze starts," Tiffany said. "Isn't it great?"

"But where did it come from?" Amy asked.

"Goliath Industries made it," Mary Ann said. "We don't know how, but it sure is fun. They said it's one of their experiments."

"Yeah," added Tiffany. "Uncle Bunkie said this is one of Goliath Industries' secret projects. He said Bicycle Hills is like a new kind of underground amusement park where you can play Caves and Cobras and other commando role-play games. They're testing it on us kids. We're really lucky to have one in Centerville."

"It's sort of like an underground cave," Amy said. "I always wanted to go into caves, but my dad never let me. Maybe it's these caves that caused the earthquake that night."

"It's more than caves," Tiffany said. "We've only gone through a few of the main passageways, but there are dozens of other trails and places like this, and each one is different. We're just discovering them. Each time you go through the window down to here it's like a new adventure. Make sure you're loaded up. Maybe we can find Sloan and the rest of our club. I've got a map."

Tiffany led the way down a hill next to the stream. Amy followed. There was a large passageway that opened up right next to where the stream disappeared. *B-1* was painted above the entrance.

"Who are we fighting?" Amy asked as they turned a corner, leaving the large room.

"Anyone who's not on the Super Wings team," Tiffany whispered. "Today our target enemy is the Cobra Club. Be careful. Once we enter this tunnel, we are out of neutral territory. Anything can happen. There are hundreds of kids down here and lots of clubs, but unless they get really lost we should only have encounters with the Cobra Club today. Tomorrow our target enemy will be the Blasters. The main thing to remember is that it's survival of the fittest down here. You'll learn the rules as we play. But if you see anyone with a red insignia patch, blast first and ask questions later. Everyone load up. Let's find Sloan so we can search for the treasure."

The dark toy weapons clicked and snapped in the girls' hands. Mary Ann showed Amy how to make sure her Faster Blaster was loaded. Amy gripped the weapon tightly.

The sense of some kind of danger made Amy feel more alive than ever. As they walked, they passed other tunnels and passageways. Usually there was a letter and a number over the entrance to each one, like C-8, D-21 and so on. At one point they heard distant voices. Amy stopped. "That's probably other teams," Tiffany reassured Amy. "We don't have to worry about them today."

The children walked on for another few minutes. The tunnel got darker and narrower. Then they heard a noise. The girls froze and listened. "I think it came from that hole," Tiffany said.

"Is it on the map?" Mary Ann asked. "I don't see any numbers."

"Must be a secret passageway," Tiffany said. "I'll check." Tiffany took a large piece of folded paper from her pocket and got the flashlight from her waist. Amy stepped closer for a better look. The map was on graph paper with letters and numbers as markings. There were swerving lines and other things. "This line here could be it," Tiffany said. "And the map says it leads to the 'Room of the Cobras.' We've never been there before. Maybe we should check it out."

"I'm with you," Diane said. "If it's a dead end, we can retrace our steps." The other girls nodded in agreement, clutching their weapons. Tiffany climbed up toward the small tunnel. The other girls were right behind her. Amy was last.

The opening of the tunnel was narrow at the beginning, but soon they could stand. Amy looked around anxiously for bugs and snakes, but the tunnels seemed free of such creatures. Amy was surprised. None of the passageways seemed like normal caves, moist and clammy and full of bats. In fact, the caves and tunnels seemed clean and neat, like the fake rocks and tunnels she had seen when she had gone to some amusement parks with her family. And there was always some light coming from somewhere. That puzzled Amy too because she never really saw light bulbs.

Then the girls stopped. They heard the sound of voices again, only this time they were louder. They walked for a short time in the dimly lit tunnel. Suddenly there was a commotion up ahead. Tiffany yelled.

"I name you prisoner!" a boy's voice said harshly. Amy immediately stepped back behind a bend in the tunnel, clutching her weapon. Her heart pounded. There were some shouts and cheers below.

"I give up," she heard Tiffany say.

"We got the rest of their team," a voice shouted. "Out, you slaves. You're prisoners of the Cobra Club now."

Amy tried to push herself back into the rock as a flashlight beam shone past her. The other girls groaned as they walked out of the tunnel. Amy waited, listening. She finally felt safe. The opposing team had missed her.

Amy held her weapon out in front of her and moved slowly forward. Her heart was beating like a drum when she got to the mouth of the tunnel. She stuck her head out slowly, looking rapidly around her. But she saw no one. The mouth of the tunnel opened into another large room which was down below Amy. Large rocks and boulders hid her from view. She heard loud voices and lots of talking. Then she heard a loud braying laugh that sounded like a sick donkey. She knew the sound of that voice—Barry Smedlowe.

Amy slowly rose up to peek over a big boulder. Down below, the Cobra Club was whooping it up over the capture of the Super Wings team. A tall cagelike structure held all the members of the Super Wings. And not only were Tiffany and the girls inside, but so were Sloan and the rest of the club. Somehow they must have been captured too. Amy couldn't understand all that they were saying because of echoes. Then all but two of the Cobra Club members marched out of the room through a passageway. The two remaining boys stood by the jail.

"They must be guards," Amy said. Then she looked down at her Faster Blaster. She knew what she had to do. She had to free the prisoners.

HIDDEN
TREASURE
· · · · · · · · ·

12

Amy took a deep breath. Then clutching her Faster Blaster, she began to crawl. Slowly she crept down through the boulders and rocks. The guards were talking and didn't see her, but Tiffany and the others did. They were trying to act casual as they whispered to each other. Amy crawled on her stomach the last thirty feet, coming to a stop behind a rock. The boys on guard were looking the other way. They were only twenty feet away. From that distance, Amy could read Tiffany's lips. She was mouthing the word *shoot* and nodding at the guards.

"I wish I knew how this gun worked," Amy thought to herself. "But it's now or never." She rose up slowly and aimed the Faster Blaster as best as she could figure out. She had shot toy guns at the fairground before, but that had been at little paper targets. Shooting at real people was another thing. Even though she knew deep down it was a game, somehow it seemed to be more than a game. The boys were so close, she didn't see how she could miss. She squinted her eyes and pulled the trigger.

The gun whooshed and made a small popping sound, like a cork gun. Almost instantly a big orange splotch of sticky glitter spread out on the back of one of the guards. The kids in the jail cheered. The other guard whirled around and Amy squeezed the trigger again. A big splotch of orange hit the boy in the chest.

"You're hit and you've been taken!" Sloan yelled. "That's a fatal hit according to the rules. Your character is dead, and Amy gets your points. Get us out of here, Amy."

Amy ran over to the wooden jail as the guard boys sat down on the ground. They were disappointed and a little angry. "I had a lot of points collected on this character," one of the guards said sadly.

"Well, you're our prisoners now," Sloan said. "We get all your point tokens. Amy, get their keys, quick. Hand over the point tokens too. We still have time to ambush the Cobra Club and get the treasure."

One of the prisoners reluctantly handed over a large key. Amy smiled as she put it in an oversized padlock. She turned the key and the lock sprang open. The kids inside the jail cheered once more. "Great work," Sloan said as he came out. He patted Amy on the back. He stood over the two slain guards as they took some gold-colored aluminum coins out of a case on their belts. The gold coins filled his hands. He then turned and gave them to Amy. "Put them in the point pouch on your belt," Sloan said, showing her which of the little compartments he meant. "You can read what the points are for later."

Sloan began acting like a general as he shouted out orders. "Let's get our weapons. We've got to go after those other guys. They got my map.

But we can stop them from getting the treasure and put those guys in their own jail. Someone needs to stand guard until we get back. I'll give extra Dream Drops and points to the ones who stay."

"I could stay," Amy said. "I still don't know much about the game yet."

"Are you kidding?" Sloan asked with a smile. "You're a good shot. I want you to come with us. Have another Dream Drop." The leader of the Super Wings opened a leather compartment on his belt and gave Amy one of the rainbow-colored candies.

Amy ate it greedily. Somehow, she did feel a surge of confidence almost immediately. The medicine taste was hardly noticeable. "I think I will go," Amy said.

"Good," Tiffany said. She patted Amy on the shoulder.

"I'll stay," Mary Ann said.

"Me too," a boy named Roger Darrow said.

Sloan nodded. Their toy weapons had been stacked against a rock. Sloan handed them quickly back to their owners. "Follow me," Sloan said. "I know a short cut."

The kids cheered and ran off down another passageway. As they formed a line, all the boys and girls congratulated Amy on being such a good shot. Amy smiled self-consciously at all the praise. This time, Amy was fourth in line in the whole group. Sloan and a boy named Billy were first. Then it was Tiffany and Amy.

"You really saved our necks," Tiffany said with a smile. "And you'll add lots of points to your character for that."

"That's right," Sloan said. "You get two kill points, besides all the points those characters had accumulated today. You'll be advancing in the game if you keep that up. You might even reach the Cobramaster level."

As they walked, Tiffany and Sloan told Amy some of the other adventures and battles the Super Wings Club had already faced since Bicycle Hills first opened. They talked so fast, Amy didn't quite understand how it all worked. But it all sounded like a lot of fun and excitement.

The Super Wings came into another large open room labeled *G-12* that was full of rocks and boulders. One large rock had several holes with water coming out of them. Something about the rock seemed vaguely familiar to Amy as she stared at it. The little separate streams fell in a row making a waterfall about three feet wide. The big stream then continued on through the middle of the room and disappeared in another tunnel.

"I think the treasure is in this room," Sloan whispered. "I wish I had my map and clue sheet. I remember that there were clues about a dripping honeycomb."

"That rock!" Amy said excitedly, pointed at the rock with all the holes. "It's shaped just like a honeycomb. And the water is falling out of it. Maybe that's it."

"You could be right," Sloan said. The group started to walk eagerly toward the rock.

"I hear voices," Tiffany whispered. Everyone stopped.

"Take cover!" Sloan hissed. "I'll tell you when to shoot."

The children scattered among the rocks and boulders like rabbits. Amy ran with Tiffany and Sloan and hid near the honeycomb rock. They had barely gotten in their places when they saw a light flash in a tunnel on the opposite side of the room. Sloan motioned for everyone to duck.

Amy scrunched low. Barry Smedlowe's voice was easy to pick out as the Cobra Club walked into the room. They talked quietly among themselves. Then someone suddenly shouted, "That rock is like a honeycomb!"

"You're right," Barry said. "Let me see the map again. I've got my clue sheet and that rat Sloan's sheet. It's like a puzzle. Mine's a picture. His clues are in words. It says the treasure is hidden where the honeycomb drips. . . ."

"Maybe it's under the waterfall," someone said.

Tiffany smiled excitedly at Amy as they listened to the kids in the

Cobra Club run across the room. Sloan peeked up carefully. He watched the group crowd around the waterfall.

"I think I see something," Barry said excitedly.

"I see it too," another boy said. "It's some kind of container."

Barry reached down through the water. "I'm getting all wet," Barry moaned. "I feel something. I've got it!" The leader of the Cobra Club yanked hard and pulled up an old metal box about twice the size of a lunch box. Amy, Tiffany and the other kids in the Super Wings Club rose up to see what was going on. The Cobra Club was so busy looking at the box, that they didn't notice that they were being watched.

"It's heavy," Barry grunted. "How does this thing open?" As Barry dragged the box away from the stream, the kids in his club gathered around. They dropped their weapons on the ground to help Barry.

Sloan raised his weapon slowly. He motioned for the others to get ready. Then Sloan brought down his arm quickly. The room was filled with whooshing and popping sounds, as Amy and the others shot their weapons. The Cobra Club yelled in surprise and fear as the glitter pellets hit. Bright orange splotches were everywhere. Amy fired two more times. The kids in the Cobra Club looked confused and bewildered as they went for their guns. One boy who already had three splotches on his uniform fired his weapon, but the others realized it was too late.

"Yahoo!" Sloan yelled. "We got them all. You can't shoot once you get a fatal hit."

Barry Smedlowe said a string of bad words and stomped his foot. He had been hit four times. "You cheated," he screamed. "How did you get out of jail?"

"We didn't cheat," Sloan said. "We just outsmarted you."

"But how?" Barry demanded. "We had your whole team locked in prison."

"You had everyone but Amy," Tiffany said, patting Amy on the back.

"Since when is she a member of your club?" Barry demanded.

"Since today," Sloan said.

"Well, I'm asking Uncle Bunkie about the rules," Barry said. "I don't think that's fair."

"Yeah," said other members in the Cobra Club. They all looked like someone had played a dirty trick on them.

"We made a fair capture, by the rules," Sloan said. "And now we'll just collect these points. And the treasure."

"We struck it rich!" Billy yelled as he opened the treasure box. Half the box was filled with paint pellets and the other half was full of the golden point coins. The boys began reading the values on the tokens.

"I'm not giving up my points to any cheaters," Barry said defiantly. "And neither is anyone in my club."

"You have to give 'em up," Sloan said. He smiled confidently, then winked at Amy.

Looking at Sloan's smiling face made Barry even more angry. He balled his hands into fists. Just then, Uncle Bunkie walked into the room.

"Ok, kids, it's time to wrap it up and get ready to go for today," the tall clown said. "I see you found the treasure. Good hunting."

"But they didn't win it fair," Barry Smedlowe whined. He ran over to Uncle Bunkie and told how his team had been unfairly tricked. Uncle Bunkie told the Cobra Club to give up their points. The Super Wings cheered. Amy helped her team collect the point tokens.

"If your team members had been thorough, they would have captured Amy also," Uncle Bunkie said. Barry had a terrible frown on his face as he poured out his fat pouch of the gold-colored tokens.

"It's no wonder they didn't see her, the sneak," Barry muttered. He glared at Amy.

"She's just smarter than you, Barry," Tiffany said and laughed. "Of course, most people are smarter than you."

Barry stepped toward Tiffany, but Sloan stepped in front of him. The two boys stood looking into each other's eyes. Sloan smiled his confident smile. He knew Barry wouldn't try anything.

"Just you wait until the next game," Barry warned. "I'll get you all. And I'll especially get you, smartie." Barry pointed a finger at Amy. Then he turned and stomped out of the room. The other kids in the Cobra Club followed.

"Sore loser," Sloan said. Then he turned to Amy. "Don't worry about him."

"I won't," Amy said confidently. She felt great. Their team had won and it was all because of her.

The Super Wings followed Uncle Bunkie through the maze of tunnels. They picked up their friends in the room of the Cobra and continued onward. Amy helped carry the treasure box part of the way. Sloan handed out Dream Drops to everyone to celebrate. Amy ate three. Maybe it was just the taste of victory, but the Dream Drops tasted the best ever. Everything seemed good and dreamy to the girl who had suddenly become a hero to her friends. She hadn't felt this good since playing on Brigadoon Farm. As she walked along, she realized that Caves and Cobras was more than just playing a game. Instead of moving pretend pieces on a board, you were in the game yourself.

Several other kids in uniforms were lined up in front of the elevator. Finally, the Super Wings had their turn. The strange blue door was open as the kids filed into the small room under the center hill. One by one they walked right through the tall window that led outside. Amy felt as if she was walking through a sheet of water when she went through the window, yet she wasn't wet.

Outside, the sun had gone down, and it was starting to get dark. Amy felt a sudden heaviness, as if she was very tired. Tiffany yawned. "I forgot all about the time," Amy said, looking at her watch. "I hope I'm not late for supper."

"Turn in your uniforms," Uncle Bunkie said.

Amy picked up her bike and pushed it through the hills to the tiny concession stand. It seemed extra heavy. She unzipped the costume and gave it to a man behind the counter. Amy hopped on the Super Wings, stood up on her pedals and zoomed toward town. By the time she got to the Centerville street, the street lights were turned on. Amy tried to pedal faster. But she felt weak and tired, and almost dizzy.

"Must be from all the excitement," she said. She sighed when she saw her father's car wasn't in the driveway. For once she was glad he was late. She parked the bike in the garage and went inside the house, hoping her stepmother wouldn't be mad.

THE PROBLEM WITH SCHOOLWORK
· · · · · · · ·

13

Amy finally began to feel as if she might like Centerville after all. After her first great performance in Caves and Cobras, she had won acceptance by the other kids in the Super Wings Club. Sloan and Tiffany were talking about making Amy some kind of officer in the club.

Amy's good game playing was also duly noted on the Big Board. She went up ten ranks to 23. Even when she wasn't playing the game, she began thinking about how she could move up. In her mind she fought fantasy battles and won fantasy victories and became a fantasy hero, saving the team, gaining a horde of points and power. It was easy to get lost in a daydream when thinking about Bicycle Hills. Like most of the kids playing the C & C game, she longed to wear the mask of the Cobramaster. From what Uncle Bunkie had hinted, a Cobramaster mask with a Trag 7 could have powers beyond belief.

Despite all this, the situations at home and at school weren't as good. Amy was still behind in her schoolwork. And the more she lagged, the more her stepmother nagged. Her father seemed disappointed when he was around, which wasn't often enough to suit Amy. Though Amy did make some efforts to keep up at school, she often got discouraged. She always felt three steps behind. She watched the clock constantly, counting down the hours and minutes. Once she got outside, she hit the bicycle racks and pedaled the shortest route to Bicycle Hills.

Her days developed into a routine. She endured school as best as possible. Then after school was over, all her friends met out at Bicycle Hills, playing as late as they could before going home for supper. On weekends, she would play all day under Bicycle Hills. Though she came out feeling tired and run down, she never felt that way when she was deep inside the Cobramaze itself.

Both her father and stepmother seemed more critical since Amy was gone so much at Bicycle Hills. Amy failed more tests and quizzes at school, and then her teacher called. Her stepmother suggested that they take the television out of Amy's room until her grades were brought up. Her father was reluctant, but her stepmother kept insisting. That night her father took the television away.

Amy was furious for several days and made a vow not to even speak to her stepmother. But it was hard to keep silent for long. Instead, Amy determined that she would just avoid her parents as much as possible. After she came home from Bicycle Hills each day, she would eat supper, go up to her room and lock the door until it was time to go to bed. She felt safe from the nagging presence of her stepmother and father. If her parents went to the country club, which was often, Amy would watch the baby and sneak in a little television, even though they had told her that she was not allowed to do so.

When her father came home late from work, Amy stopped going downstairs to greet him if she was in her room. If they asked her questions, she said she was doing homework and working on her geography project, which was only partially true.

Amy hated opening her text books. By the time supper was over, she was often tired. Every moment of studying was a struggle. She was especially worried about the big geography project. She had to prepare reports on every South American country. The reports seemed like a mountain of work, and Amy didn't know where to start. So she didn't. Like a lot of her schoolwork, she let it slide, promising herself she'd get to it in time to turn it in.

As she sat at her desk intending to study, she would find herself reading the same page over and over and not remembering any of it. She kept a supply of Rainbow Dream Drops in her desk drawers at school and home. She usually sucked on one or two as she tried to do her homework. The taste reminded her of being under Bicycle Hills. Even though there was always the bad medicine taste for a moment, it didn't last long and was worth the unpleasantness. Sucking on one of the candies made it easy to drift off into a daydream about playing the game. Just thinking and pretending she was playing C & C was a lot more fun than trying to concentrate on boring schoolwork.

The October days rushed on. The homework problem hit home on a Friday, the week before Halloween. Amy had turned in her geography project and gotten an F. Her teacher called again. That evening, her father and stepmother talked privately in their bedroom before going to the country club. Amy thought that was a bad sign. On Saturday morning, they called Amy into the living room to talk. Amy sat down, feeling tense.

"Your teacher says you'll be receiving failing grades on three subjects when your report card comes out," her father said slowly.

"I'll do better," Amy said defensively. "Don't you remember that I started out behind? I can catch up if I just try a little harder."

"But you haven't caught up," her stepmother said. Amy glared at her.

"Jane is right," her dad said. "We've been discussing Bicycle Hills also. We're concerned about how much time you spend out there. Somehow it doesn't seem healthy."

"That's right," Mrs. Burke added. "You look as pale as a ghost, except for the times you've been sneaking makeup out of my bathroom."

Amy looked surprised. She didn't think her stepmother had noticed. Amy had started using the makeup a week ago when Tiffany had suggested she use it to be like the other girls. "I'd buy my own makeup if you'd let me," Amy said. "You don't want me to do anything that's fun."

"We're not here to talk about makeup," her father said. "We are discussing Bicycle Hills."

"Your teacher and some parents are concerned about that place," Mrs. Burke said. "Just exactly what do you do there?"

"We ride our bikes and play games," Amy said uneasily. "It's a lot of fun."

"What kind of games?" her father asked.

"Just games of pretend," Amy said slowly. "Sort of like cops and robbers or tag. Does it matter?"

"We think perhaps you're spending too much time playing with your friends," Mrs. Burke said, her voice sounding unsure. Amy's father and stepmother looked at each other and then back at her.

"At least I get home for supper, don't I?" Amy said defiantly. "Besides, it's no different than you going to the country club every other night. You spend most of your time working and the rest at the club."

"That's not being fair," her stepmother snapped. "Your father's been working hard, and he needs time to unwind and let the stress out."

"He used to unwind taking walks with me," Amy said.

"You can't be expecting to monopolize your dad's time," Mrs. Burke replied. "He's an important businessman in an important organization, and he's heading up in the world. He needs to be in those meetings not only to relax but for business reasons too. It's not all fun and games."

"Well, if I don't spend enough time at Bicycle Hills, I'll get behind," Amy countered. "I'm doing better at my rank in the Point System, and I need to be playing to keep up my good scores. I never had this high a rank before. This is the score that really matters, isn't it?" Amy held up her dark number card so they could see the big number 23. "I would think that you would be proud of me instead of bothering me all the time about schoolwork. I'll catch up pretty soon."

"Well, it's true that your Point System scores are the best they've been," her father said reluctantly.

"But there's more to life than a good rank in the Point System,' her stepmother quickly added.

"What else is there?" Amy asked. "That's the point, isn't it? To go as high as you can in the Point System? Isn't that fulfilling your potential like you've been bugging me about?"

"I don't think it's fair to say we're bugging you," her father said stiffly. "We try to encourage you, that's all."

"When we took the television out of your room, we hoped that would take away the temptation not to study," her stepmother said. "But apparently that's not enough. Your father suggested we remove your music rack too."

"Not my music," Amy blurted out. "That's not fair."

"But I thought we should take another approach," Mrs. Burke said. "I think, I mean, your father and I think that you're just spending too much time out at Bicycle Hills. So until your grades improve, we think you should stop going there. In fact, we forbid you to go. Isn't that right, Richard?"

"That's what we decided, Amy," her father said slowly. "No more Bicycle Hills for a while."

"You can't," Amy yelled out. "You just can't do that to me. Take my music if you want it. Don't let her do that to me, Daddy. I am doing better in the Point System. Give me a chance to bring up my grades."

Amy looked frantically at her father to see what he would say, but he looked down at the floor. Her father seemed confused and upset. "Well, maybe we should give her some more time," her father said to his wife. "Maybe we could just take the music out of her room, and then if . . ."

"Richard, you said we would be firm and act together on this," she said shrilly. "I don't see why you should take her side in this matter. I hope you don't intend to show this kind of favoritism often. What will happen when little Sarah Jane gets older and sees you sticking up for Amy? It seems you would choose against both of us to spoil this child."

"I'm not choosing sides," Dr. Burke said.

"Well, you certainly aren't backing me up in the matter," Mrs. Burke said. "If you don't want Amy to respect me, then I don't know how you expect me to be her mother."

"You're not my mother," Amy blurted out. "My real mother would never act like you."

"Why you ungrateful child, after all I've done to . . ."

Just then the baby began to wail in the other room. Mrs. Burke turned away from Amy and walked quickly out of the room. The anger hung in the air like thick fog. Amy felt she couldn't breathe. She looked into her father's eyes. Suddenly he looked old and sad and tired.

"Why didn't you defend me?" Amy asked.

"Amy, you know how much I care about you," her father said.

"I'm not sure what I know," Amy said in disgust. Tears began to fill her eyes. "I'm going out to ride my bike." Amy stood up and walked away. More than anything she kept hoping that her father would call to her as she headed to the door, but he didn't. The tears were streaming down her face as she opened the door. She found her bicycle in a blur. There was still a spark of hope that he would still call her back and take her in his arms like he used to so she could cry out all the frustration and hurt. But he didn't call her name. She felt at that moment as if her father had died, maybe not the same way her mother had died, but he was still gone. Amy had never felt more lonely in all her life. She swallowed her sobs and wiped her eyes with her arm.

Amy wasn't sure what to do. She wanted to run away, to get on her bike and pedal out of Centerville and just keep going. But she knew she couldn't. And she knew she wasn't supposed to go to Bicycle Hills. But she didn't want to go back home. After a moment, she rode to the library. For a while she looked at books on biology and cells. It reminded of her of the good old days when she and her father used to take nature walks on Brigadoon Farm. Those days seemed gone forever to the girl.

"Nothing lasts," Amy muttered. She looked out the window. Out on the street, a crowd of kids rode by on big red bicycles. They were laughing and yelling. Amy sat up straighter when she saw John Kramar. She wished he would stop and talk to her. But the mob of kids pedaled on down the street. She wondered where they were going. They looked so happy and free to the miserable girl.

Amy sat still, remembering the night of the fire and seeing the chains and the place they called the kingdom. Suddenly, she felt uneasy. She went into the bathroom and turned on the water. She splashed it on her face. Then she pulled a paper towel from the machine near the sink. As she dried the cool water, she looked at herself in the mirror. She was surprised how white and pale her face appeared. The rims of her eyelids seemed especially red. "Must be the light in here," Amy muttered. She left the bathroom quickly, and almost ran down the library steps.

She was just getting on her bike when she saw Tiffany riding quickly down the street. "Amy, where have you been?" Tiffany asked urgently as she coasted to a stop. "We needed you this morning. We had an absolute disaster. Where were you?"

Amy quickly told her about her argument with her parents. Tiffany seemed totally sympathetic and understanding. "You poor thing," Tiffany said. "How can they do that?"

"It's more my stepmother than my dad," Amy said. "Nothing I do pleases her. My dad just goes along with her. When he's home, that is."

"Well, I don't know what we're going to do without you," Tiffany said. "Halloween is less than a week away now. And you should have been there. Barry and his club ambushed our team but good. We had just gotten our best treasure haul yet and were hiding in the place we discovered last week. All our treasure and tokens and everything was hidden there. But when we got there today, we were ambushed by the Cobra Club."

"You're kidding," Amy said. "How did he know?"

"That rat Roger Darrow betrayed us," Tiffany said. "I never trusted him. Apparently, Barry bought him off somehow and he led them right to our hideout. They blasted us good. I've never seen Sloan so mad. I thought he would start beating up Roger. But the other guys on the club held him back."

"You mean we're not in the lead to be the winners on Halloween?" Amy asked.

"Nope," Tiffany said. "We'll be lucky if we even come close. Barry and the Cobra Club are way ahead in points and tokens and treasure and everything. That's why we need your help."

"But I can't play," Amy said. "I told you what happened."

"I don't mean that kind of help," Tiffany said solemnly.

"What help then?" Amy asked.

"We need the Trag 7," Tiffany said. "You can get one and we need it. Now more than ever."

"But how will that help?" Amy asked.

"Well, it was a secret, but two days ago Sloan cashed in a lot of points and tokens and got a special C & C manual from Uncle Bunkie," Tiffany said in a whisper. "The manual tells about how to use the Trag 7. I have never seen him so excited. He didn't tell me how it worked. But after this morning's disaster, he told me to find you. He said getting a Trag 7 is our only hope now to win on Halloween."

"But how can we win back all those points?" Amy asked.

"I'm not sure how we'll do it, but we've got to trust Sloan," Tiffany said. "Otherwise we don't have a chance."

Amy looked at her friend. She suddenly wondered if Tiffany was telling her the whole truth. Something about the popular girl's manner seemed secretive. Tiffany smiled to reassure her.

"Can the club count on you or not?" Tiffany asked.

"When do you need it?" Amy asked. "And for how long?"

"Not until Halloween night," Tiffany said. "We'll only be borrowing it that night, I promise."

Amy thought for a moment. She saw her dad and stepmother and the scene of their argument that morning. "Ok, I'll try to get it," Amy said. "I can't promise anything, but I'll try."

"Great," Tiffany said. "But this has to remain an absolute secret. No one, not even other kids in the club can know. Only you, me and Sloan."

Amy nodded. She could see the strange black box in her mind. And as she saw it, a plan began to form.

SECRET
MISSION
· · · · · · · · ·
14

Amy waited all that weekend to get a Trag 7
box, but there wasn't a chance. After talking to Tiffany, she had gone
home and searched every corner, drawer and shelf in her father's office,
but found nothing. Though she felt guilty about being a sneak, she was
still mad at her father and stepmother. "He deserves it," Amy muttered
to herself as she looked in the drawers and closets. But deep inside, she
wasn't quite so sure. From what her father had told her about the boxes,
they sounded like they could be dangerous. But that couldn't be right,
Amy reasoned, or why else would the winners of the Caves and Cobras
game receive the Trag 7's rewards? Surely Goliath Industries wouldn't

give the children something bad or dangerous.

But Amy wondered about Goliath. She had thought more and more about the warnings of John and Susan Kramar and Daniel Bayley. They seemed to think Goliath was going to do something awful on Halloween. And Amy had heard Cyrus Cutright and Uncle Bunkie say some odd things that time she had hidden in her father's office. But what did it all prove? She sighed and kept looking for the Trag 7 box, not really sure she would take it if she found it. But she never had to face that decision since she never saw the mysterious black box. Amy was almost relieved that she couldn't find it.

At school on Monday, the other children in the Super Wings Club seemed discouraged about their horrible defeat at the hands of Barry Smedlowe. The members of the Cobra Club, as expected, were absolutely gloating about their great victory. The only one who seemed unaffected was Sloan Favor. He didn't look happy or sad. Just determined. He approached Amy at lunch time. He nodded his head so they could talk at the end of the long lunch table in private. Amy felt privileged and important that she was singled out by the older boy. She could see that the other girls in her class were watching her. Sloan smiled and stared at her silently. His blue eyes looked like crystal lakes, Amy thought.

"Tiffany said you couldn't find the box," Sloan said.

"I tried my best," Amy said. "Dad's not bringing them home anymore."

"The whole club is counting on you," Sloan said seriously. "You've got to get one by Halloween. Maybe you could go to his office."

"I have to be home right after school each day for two weeks," Amy said. "They want to make sure I don't go to Bicycle Hills."

"Well, keep checking," Sloan said. "We'll have to think of something. In the meantime I'll make sure we have the necessary ingredients to make the Trag 7 unit work. I found out a few things in the secret manual."

"What makes them work?" Amy asked.

"I better not say for now," he said with a mysterious smile. "All I can say is that I need to go hunting this week. Bird hunting." With another perfect smile, Sloan left the table. Amy wondered what he meant, though something about birds did seem familiar. Then she remembered—her father had all those birds in his office. She thought there might be a connection, but what? None of it made much sense to her.

The rest of that week passed slowly for Amy. Every evening, her parents went to the country club, which meant she had to baby-sit little Sarah Jane. Since the town elections were coming up the week after Halloween, the ORDER political party was making a big push. But that was only part of the reason for so many meetings. Goliath was also throwing a big party for the adults on Halloween night at the country club. And while the adults were having their party, the kids were promised a party too, in another part of the country club. The plan was to have the kids play over at Bicycle Hills and then come across the road and watch a scary movie at the country club. Goliath officials didn't say the children would be playing Caves and Cobras, only that there would be games. That sounded fine to all the parents because they were looking for ways to keep their children off the streets on Halloween night.

Amy's father had seemed more worried and distant than ever that week. Amy thought it was because of their argument on Saturday. On Wednesday evening he came home and seemed very upset. Amy stood outside their bedroom door as they got ready to go to the club so she could listen.

"You don't think it will really turn into an all-out war, do you?" her stepmother asked.

"It looks very bad," he said. "The government has even put a ban on the news reports so people won't panic. But Mr. Cutright seemed to know what he was talking about."

Their voices faded away as they walked into the bathroom. Amy continued to listen, but couldn't make out the words. Her father sounded scared. After they left for the country club, Amy turned on the television.

She found a station with news. The newscasters looked grim, but they didn't say anything that sounded new. They talked about countries fighting and terrorists and all the people out of work. Then they talked about elections. Amy turned to another channel.

Later that evening, Amy was still awake when her father and stepmother came home. Her father was loud and bumped into things. Amy could tell without looking that he had been drinking again. He had come home several times like that in the last few weeks. It made Amy mad and scared. But that night, he had started crying in the hall—just like a child. Amy got out of bed. She opened her door, but her stepmother was already taking him into the bedroom. "Everything's all right," her stepmother said when she saw Amy. "Go back to bed."

Amy had trouble falling asleep. Through the walls she could hear her father still moaning and crying.

Before school on Thursday, the day before Halloween, Tiffany met Amy at the bicycle racks. She was smiling and looked excited. "We have a plan," Tiffany said. "Sloan thought of it while he was bird hunting."

"Bird hunting?" Amy asked. "Why is he doing that?"

"You'll find out soon enough," Tiffany said. "The main thing is that we get a Trag 7 unit."

"I go into my dad's study each night and I just can't find one," Amy said. "He's not bringing any home."

"But he does have them at work, right?" Tiffany asked.

"Yes, I suppose," Amy replied.

"So we get one from his office," Tiffany replied. "Sloan had a great idea. All you need is the key to your dad's office."

"But when would I go there?" Amy asked. "I have to go right home after school. And I'll have to baby-sit again tonight. My parents are on the Halloween party committee."

"That's what Sloan figured," Tiffany said. "That's why we plan to go down there around midnight. And you're coming with us. You can sneak out of your house and meet us outside. Only you've got to get the key to your dad's office. That's important."

Tiffany walked with Amy inside the school telling her more about the secret plan. At first, Amy thought it wouldn't work. But the more she listened to the details, the more she thought they might have a chance. Since Mr. Favor was the executive vice president at the plant, Sloan had found out a way to get a key to a little-used back gate. He also had a plan to get inside the office building. The whole scheme frightened and intrigued Amy.

"It'll be an adventure, just like going on a C & C mission," Tiffany whispered at lunch. "We can be in and out in no time. And we use the same plan to return the unit the next night. He probably won't work on Saturday. He'll never miss it. We've got to have a Trag 7 to win the game. You can't let the club down."

After school, Amy told Tiffany she would try to get her dad's office key. Tiffany slapped her on the back. "Meet me at ten minutes to midnight in front of our house," Tiffany said.

Amy was fidgety that evening. Her father seemed pale and sickly that night at supper. Amy figured it was from drinking. Getting the key turned out to be simpler than she figured. He took fairly long showers. So while he was in the bathroom, Amy walked quietly in the bedroom. His keys were on the dresser in a leather pouch. There were only four keys. Two kinds of car keys, the house key and another key. Amy slipped the last key off its hook and walked out of the room.

She was nervous that he would notice the missing key, but they left for the country club without a word. They came home around ten-thirty. Her father sounded like he'd been drinking again, but at least he wasn't crying, Amy thought to herself.

Amy forced herself to stay awake. Once she was sure her stepmother had closed their bedroom door for the night, Amy got dressed in her school clothes. She turned on her lamp to read a novel. The book was good and she was nervous, so she didn't really get too tired. At fifteen minutes before twelve, Amy turned off the lamp and headed downstairs.

Her stepmother was a light sleeper, especially since little Sarah Jane had been born. So Amy tiptoed down the stairs. She went through the kitchen door into the garage and out the side door. Her Super Wings bicycle was waiting there. So was Tiffany.

"Did you get the key?"

"I got it," Amy replied.

"Then let's go. Sloan's already out at the factory."

Both girls pedaled quickly and quietly down the streets. The October night was cooler than Amy had expected. She wished she had worn a heavier sweater or jacket. The Centerville streets were quiet. Amy was glad they didn't meet any cars. Once they got out of town, the moon was almost full and lit up Cemetery Road for them. When they got to the big chain-link fence that surrounded the factory, Tiffany turned off the asphalt and coasted down onto a field. By the fence was a small dirt road that Amy had never noticed before. They followed the fence all the way down until it turned a corner. Sloan was waiting in the moonlight. A small fenced gate was open.

"She got the key," Tiffany whispered. Sloan smiled.

"Great," he said, patting Amy on the back. "Let's go."

They pedaled across the factory grounds toward the big buildings. When they got close, they hid their bikes behind a large truck. Though there were a lot of lights on around the buildings, Sloan led them in such a way that they avoided being too much in the open. Amy felt both scared and excited as they ran hiding behind things. In no time, they arrived at a door at the back of the office building. Two big garbage dumpsters were just outside the door.

"This is a door the janitors use," Sloan said. He smiled as he held up a key. He quickly opened the door, and the children moved inside. Amy's heart was pounding as they ran down the quiet hallways. At night, in the building all alone, the dimly lit hallways seemed eerie. Sloan led them right to her father's office door. Amy fitted the key. The lock wouldn't turn. Then she heard a click. Sloan pushed the door open.

They shut it quietly. Tiffany turned on a light.

Everything looked the same. "Let's look in the lab." Amy said. The other two followed her. When Amy flipped on the light, she almost screamed when she heard something move and squeak.

"Birds," Sloan said. He looked at the cages of sparrows. "If I had known we could have gotten a bird too, I wouldn't have had to hunt all week. I almost broke my neck climbing around the rafters in an old abandoned barn to catch a sparrow."

"What do you need a bird for?" Amy asked.

"You'll find out," Sloan replied. "Let's get a Trag 7."

Amy saw several aluminum cases under a large stone lab table. She bent over and pulled one out. She unfastened the latches.

"You found one!" Tiffany said. Sloan had already opened another case. There was a Trag 7 in it too. He stared at it and then closed the lid. He picked up the aluminum case.

"Let's go," he said. "We'll take two units."

"But you said you just wanted one," Amy said in surprise. "You can't take two."

"What's the difference?" Sloan said. "We can return them both Saturday. What if one doesn't work? We need to be sure."

Before Amy could argue, Tiffany took the case Amy was holding. "Wait," Amy said. But Tiffany had shut the lid of the case and was following her brother. Amy ran after them. Sloan was already out in the hallway. Amy flipped off the light in the lab and the one in the office. She made sure the door was locked. Sloan and Tiffany were both waiting down at the end of the hallway. Sloan waved his arm for her to come. Amy muttered to herself and ran down the hall. She was afraid to talk in the building. And once they were outside with the door locked, Amy figured it was too late to change Sloan's mind. She looked down at her watch. It was fifteen minutes past midnight. Halloween had begun.

The children ran toward their bikes. This time they weren't trying to be so secretive. Up in the office building, Cyrus Cutright and Uncle Bunkie the clown looked out a window, watching the three children get on their bikes and ride off into the darkness.

"That Favor boy works fast," Uncle Bunkie said.

"He's like his father," Cyrus Cutright said and chuckled. "He knows how to follow orders."

"I wasn't sure the girl would come through," Uncle Bunkie said. "I suggested to the boy what he might try, in a roundabout way, of course."

"You coached him well," the old man said. "And you've done a good job with the Smedlowe boy, also."

"He's a greedy one," the big clown grunted. "He can hardly wait for the Final Game."

"You'll be rewarded for your efforts," Mr. Cutright said. "Now that the children are set, a few details remain for the Halloween parties. It's time to increase the dosage in the Rainbow Dream Drops. I'll have a stronger batch taken over by the afternoon."

"I thought we already reached the limits on those," Uncle Bunkie.

"Halloween is special," the old man said. "We have permission this year to do more than you or I have ever seen. We want a good dose in the candy. After all, we want them to have a good time, don't we?"

"Sweet dreams!" the big clown said with a grin. "Everything they've been pretending will finally come true. It will be a night never forgotten in the history of this miserable little town."

"And in the whole world," the old thin man added. "I can hardly wait to eat the ashes on this one."

The two men laughed and laughed until their eyes glowed red.

Amy was sure they had gotten away without being noticed. Everything had seemed so easy. Her fears about taking the two boxes had almost gone by the time they pulled up in front of the Favor's house. Tiffany and Sloan had both assured her that they would be able to return the Trag 7 units easily, maybe even that same night after the Halloween party. Amy decided it was all going to be ok.

"Meet us at seven-thirty sharp by the window in Bicycle Hills," Sloan said. "We'll group up in the Nesting Den as usual. I want you to be there when we unleash the secret weapon."

"Weapon?" Amy asked.

"All it takes is the blood of a wild bird," Tiffany said, her eyes shone like they were hungry.

"Don't tell our secrets," Sloan warned his sister.

"The blood of a wild bird?" Amy asked.

Sloan turned without saying another word and pedaled up the driveway. Tiffany followed.

Still wondering about wild birds, Amy parked her bike by the side door on the garage and went inside. She went into the house, glad the night's adventure was over without a mistake. That's when the kitchen light flipped on.

"So there you are!" her stepmother said. "You've been gone for over forty minutes. Where have you been?"

HALLOWEEN
NIGHT
· · · · · · · · ·
15

Amy couldn't believe that she was
stuck at home on Halloween night. All her friends were going to be out
having fun at Bicycle Hills when she had risked her neck so Sloan and
Tiffany could get the Trag 7. Her stepmother had been furious with Amy.
She had almost called the police, she said. No matter how many questions she had asked, all Amy said was that she had been out riding her
bicycle around with some friends. She was sorry she had even mentioned her friends because when she wouldn't say who they were, her
stepmother had really gotten mad.

Mrs. Burke was still upset at breakfast time. That's when she told

Amy's father. He had looked at Amy with surprise and dismay. Amy almost felt glad she had been caught when she saw the look on his face. Her stepmother had insisted that Amy be forbidden to go out on Halloween. And that was just the first part of her punishment. She thought there should be more, but Dr. Burke had to leave because he was late for work. Luckily, Amy had been able to put his key back in the key pouch without being caught.

When Amy had told Tiffany at school what had happened, her neighbor didn't seem bothered or sad. Amy was surprised.

"We'll miss you," Tiffany had said. When Amy said it would be hard for her to get out to return the Trag 7 units, Tiffany told her not to worry, that she and Sloan would take care of it. But she wouldn't really say how or when they would do it, which worried Amy.

"Just quit bothering me with all these questions," Tiffany had finally snapped at Amy at lunch time. "You act like a big baby. Why don't you just grow up or shut up?"

"Yeah," Mary Ann grunted. "You are acting like a real child." The other kids got up from the table, leaving Amy sitting all by herself. Tears of frustration and anger came to her eyes.

"You would think they would care a little about what happened to me," she thought to herself. "But all they want is that stupid box." The more Amy thought about it, the more used she felt. More than ever, she wished she could just run away and go where there were no people. "People always let you down and disappoint you," she thought. "I'll just live without friends. I can get by. I don't need anybody, and they don't need me." She reached in her pocket automatically for her Dream Drops, but her pocket was empty. In disgust, Amy stomped out of the cafeteria, convinced that it was the worst day of her life.

And the day didn't get any better. That night, when all the kids in town were out having fun on Halloween, Amy was sitting at home feeling sorry for herself, especially when the baby started crying. She was about to explode, trying to think of things to do to make the baby happy. She did everything but stand on her head, and she was about to try that when the baby just suddenly got tired and fell asleep. Amy put her down in the playpen and went down to the television.

She turned on a Halloween movie about some kids and a haunted house. She got a bowl of ice cream from the refrigerator and went back to the movie. Just as the music got really creepy, the movie suddenly stopped. There was a hum and then a message flashed on the screen.

EMERGENCY BULLETIN!!
PLEASE STAND BY!!

Amy waited. Then a very serious-looking man appeared. He was one of the men who told the news each night. Amy wasn't sure, but this man almost looked frightened, as if he had been watching a scary movie too.

"We interrupt your regular viewing schedule to give a special report," the announcer said. "Peace talks and negotiations broke down in Geneva earlier this evening as tempers flared over the controversial ORDER political party proposal to bring unity among the participating nations. While the talks were taking place, a surprise attack in Israel triggered a reaction from the three superpower nations—the United States, the Soviet Union and the nation of China. There have been rumors, not yet confirmed, that three United States military bases, one in Europe, one in Spain and one in the Philippines have been attacked. No one is sure if these are terrorist attacks or attacks by another nation. There have been other rumors that an attack of greater proportions might be planned for the mainland of the United States itself. These are only rumors however. In a moment, we will hear a message from the President of the United States."

Amy stopped eating her ice cream and watched. The doorbell rang again. She jumped up startled. She ran for the door. She was very surprised to see John Kramar standing there on the front walk. Next to him was his big old red Spirit Flyer bicycle. "We've got to talk," John said seriously. "Some real bad things are about to happen, we think, and we need your help."

"You mean the news about the bombings on TV?" Amy asked.

"What do you mean?" John asked.

"Come see," Amy said. They both ran into the living room. The screen was all fuzzy. Amy turned the channels. All the channels were the same.

"That's odd," Amy said. "It seems like our television is broken. They were saying something about rumors of wars."

"There is a war going on," John said. "And another battle is about to start right now over at Bicycle Hills. You've got to come with me and help us stop it before it's too late."

"What do you mean?" Amy asked.

"Let me show you," John said. "Come outside." Amy looked once more at the television, made sure the baby was ok and then went out to the sidewalk by the front door. "You can see it in the mirror if you look closely," John said.

"But that mirror is broken," Amy replied. The mirror on the old red Spirit Flyer had a sliver of glass in it, but most of it was gone.

"Just look into the part of the mirror that's there," John said. "I'll turn it to face the other way."

"Why do you do that?" Amy asked. "Why don't you use it the normal way?"

"Because in the normal way it's a rearview mirror and only looks back in time, but turned toward the front, it can reflect the future."

"You're kidding!" Amy said. "Is this some kind of Halloween trick?"

"I'm not kidding," John said. "All the kids with Spirit Flyers have been trying to figure out what Goliath was up to in Bicycle Hills. But we didn't really see it until today. We were out playing a game of flight tag when it happened. It took all our bikes with the lights and mirrors. It's hard to explain, but the thing is, you can see it in my mirror if you'll just look."

Amy nodded. Something inside told her not to be too skeptical. She had already seen that the old bike could do very unusual things. And for the first time in a long time, she was almost glad to see John and his strange old bike. She was lonely and he had at least always been friendly to her. Even if he was a bit strange, at least he seemed honest and nice. She watched as he carefully twisted the old broken mirror so it faced the front of the bike.

"Get close so you can see it."

Amy felt a little foolish, but she leaned forward to look into the cracked glass. "All I see is my face, ' Amy said. That's when John reached down and pressed the gear lever forward. Amy jumped back. Right before her eyes, the image in the mirror changed. At first things seemed fuzzy and odd. But then she saw deeper into the situation. Bicycle Hills came into view. Then the scene changed, and something like an odd kind of movie or video seemed to be playing on the piece of mirror. The mirror showed walls and tunnels that looked like those down under Bicycle Hills. Some children were creeping through the tunnel in their C & C commando uniforms. Then Amy recognized the children. It was the Super Wings Club, with Sloan and Tiffany at the head of the line. That's when Amy saw the Trag 7 box in Sloan's hands.

"The Trag 7," Amy said, pointing. "How could your bike know about it? That's supposed to be a secret."

"You call that box a Trag 7?" John asked. "We think that's the cause of the problems. Daniel Bayley's seen one before. He says they're powerful, but he doesn't know much about them or how they work. But that's only one reason why the kids are in trouble."

"What trouble?" Amy asked.

The scene in the mirror changed. Then Amy saw people in their C & C uniforms. They were running and looked afraid. Amy thought they were probably in a battle in one of the games, but then she saw something else, something that made her catch her breath. Coming out of one of the tunnels were two large red eyes, bigger than garbage-pail lids. Amy gasped when she saw that the eyes belonged to a snake—a snake bigger than any snake she had ever seen. The gigantic reptile slithered into the room and filled it. The head of the snake spread. Then Amy realized it looked exactly like a giant cobra with a head as big as a house.

Suddenly, the mouth of the snake opened. She expected to see a large tongue come out of the dark mouth, but instead, it looked as if people wearing a type of C & C uniform were walking out of the reptile's mouth. Only these creatures walked stiffly, almost like robots.

"Those are Daimones," John said.

"Who?" Amy asked.

"Daimones," John replied. "They are creatures from the Deeper World and they're up to no good. They're more or less the same as those snakey-looking guards on the corners of the walls at Bicycle Hills. They take different forms, but they're all evil."

The next thing the mirror showed was a scene of children struggling with dark chains. Amy felt a sinking feeling in her stomach when she realized that she had seen those same kind of chains before. Then she saw herself. Only this wasn't a reflection. She was in the crowd. "I'm in the picture too," Amy cried out. "But look at me!"

Chains were on her hands, and she was being dragged with the rest. Then the mirror went back to normal. Amy saw her pale face looking back at herself. Then even that changed. Her face was covered in a shadow. But the shadow was changing. Amy stepped back when she saw what looked like dark shadowy scales all over her skin. They seemed so real, as if her skin were even made of shadows. Amy jerked back, but she couldn't stop staring at her reflection. That's when she saw the chain connected to a dark metal ring around her neck.

"Stop!" Amy cried out. She turned away and hid her face in her hands and began to cry. She couldn't stop the tears. She felt embarrassed. Part of her was just afraid, and part of her felt terribly lonely. Yet there was something deeper inside, and it had to do with the chain and the time she had seen the Kingson and the kingdom. Deep down, she knew she should have used the golden key that night and gotten rid of the chain.

But it seemed too late for that now. And that was the sorrow she felt. She was now too deep in a mess. She had stolen the Trag 7 boxes and lied to her parents and done awful things. It seemed hopeless and too late to do anything. She buried her face in her hands.

She wasn't sure how long she had cried, but she felt John's arm around her. "It's ok," John said. "We won't see any more right now. But we've seen other things, stuff that looks horrible with those Daimones and the kids down in those caves."

"I helped get that box to Sloan," Amy said sadly, wiping her nose with her sleeve. She paused, thinking. "In fact they have two of them."

"Two of them?" John asked. "We only saw one in the mirrors."

"They were only supposed to use one," Amy said. "Our team was going to use it to win the games tonight. Whoever wins gets their own Trag 7 box. They can do really strange things." Amy quickly told John what she knew about the odd black boxes as John listened patiently. "We were only going to borrow them, then return them tomorrow," Amy said.

"You have to get them back, or I think something awful is going to happen," John said. "Everyone who plays in Bicycle Hills tonight is in danger. Goliath has something planned. There's something different in the air too. You can sense it even without a Spirit Flyer. I have a bad feeling about tonight."

"They were talking about some bad things on the television," Amy said slowly. She stared at the old red bike. "Every time I'm around these old bikes something strange happens. I don't know who to trust anymore. Everyone is out to trick you, it seems."

"There is a trick being played, but it's not by us," John said firmly. "You've seen at least part of the kingdom. You know what a Spirit Flyer can do. Have we ever hurt you or said anything untrue? The only trick being played is by Goliath and ORDER companies. And they're doing it right now to all your friends. I think you're the only one that can stop them. You got them the boxes, so you can get them back. That's the way it works. But you have to take action. They won't listen to us. We already tried to talk to Sloan before he went into Bicycle Hills. He just called us names and threw a rock at Daniel. If you go down there, maybe they will listen to you."

"But what about the baby?" Amy said. "I just can't leave her."

"Where are your parents?"

"They're at the party at the country club."

"Wrap her up and let's go then," John said. "We'll go on the Spirit Flyer. Hurry, we haven't got any time to lose."

"I guess I could," Amy said. She wiped the last tears from her eyes. For a moment she felt like maybe it wasn't too late. "But then I'll have to tell Dad I took the Trag 7 units. I'll really be in trouble then."

"There's going to be a lot worse trouble if you don't tell him," John said. "Let's go. Get your jacket and wrap up the baby."

As Amy went to get her jacket in her room, she reached in her desk drawer to get her keys. As she put them in her pocket, she remembered something. She dropped down to the floor and looked under her bed. The golden key with the three crowns was still there. Amy reached under the bed and picked up the odd key. She had ignored it ever since she had kicked it under the bed. So much had happened since then. Something about holding the heavy golden key made Amy feel better inside. Not being sure why, she put the key in her pocket. Somehow, she felt that she was supposed to take it with her.

Amy was amazed little Sarah Jane didn't cry when she picked her up. She wrapped the baby tight in the blanket and locked the door. No sooner had she climbed on the back of the old red bicycle than John began pedaling. "Be careful," Amy said. "I've got the baby."

John nodded and pushed the handlebars so they pointed upward. The big balloon tires left the driveway before the bike hit the street. John rode about four feet off the pavement until he passed the first street light, then the old bike began a slow climb into the night air. They shot right over the top of the Baker's house and went higher. The lights from the factory and the country club came into view and John pedaled faster.

The old bike zipped quickly and quietly through the air. Something about being on the Spirit Flyer this time was less frightening to Amy. Little Sarah Jane was still soundly asleep in her arms, unaware that she was over a hundred feet off the ground.

As John came in over the country-club grounds, the bike began to descend. When they got to the back of the club, John hit the brake. The Spirit Flyer stopped in midair before slowly dropping down to the ground. Amy hopped off. "Wait for me," she said. She ran toward the nearest door.

As Amy carried little Sarah inside the main clubhouse room, things seemed awfully confusing to the girl. There were people everywhere in the large room, dancing or sitting at little tables with drinks and food. Some people were dressed in costumes. Then she saw her parents at a table near the door. "Daddy!" Amy yelled. Dr. Burke looked up. He seemed puzzled when he saw Amy. Amy's stepmother looked confused, then angry, then concerned when she saw Amy had little Sarah Jane.

"Amy, what are you doing here?" Dr. Burke asked. "You should be home."

"I took two of those boxes. I'm sorry, Daddy. We planned to return them. Honest we did," Amy blurted out. Mrs. Burke took the baby from Amy's arms. Her father pulled Amy over to a hallway where it was more quiet. Across the room, Mr. Cyrus Cutright had been watching Amy talking to her father. The old man frowned.

"Now slow down and tell me from the beginning," Dr. Burke said. Amy quickly told the whole story about why she had taken the boxes. She thought she would break down and cry again, but she didn't. As she talked, a serious look came over her father's face.

"Amy, those boxes are top secret. You children shouldn't be playing with them," Dr. Burke said. "You probably couldn't do too much damage with one. Still, I don't understand how you could do such a thing."

"Sloan said they were going to do something with it," Amy added.

"He said they were going to use blood. The blood of a wild bird and . . ." Mr. Burke's face suddenly went pale. He stared at Amy, speechless.

Finally he said, "We've got to stop your friends right now. I'm going with you." Dr. Burke stood up straight. He almost bumped into Mr. Cutright.

"Things are heating up. We need you for an emergency meeting right now," the old thin man said. "It's happening. It's already on the news. The stations are coming through. The President has . . ." The old man stopped, stared at Amy, then leaned forward and whispered something into Dr. Burke's ear.

"So we need you right now," Mr. Cutright said.

Amy thought her father looked confused. Sweat had popped out on his forehead. He suddenly looked afraid, almost like the announcer on the television earlier. He bent over and held Amy by her shoulders. "Listen carefully," Dr. Burke said. "I want you to find your friends and get those boxes back now. Do you understand? It's extremely important."

"Something else is happening, isn't it?" Amy asked, suddenly growing afraid. "They were talking about attacks on the television but then the reception messed up."

"Go get those boxes," her father said. Without another word, he turned and walked out of the room with Mr. Cutright. Amy watched her father walk away. Then she ran for the door.

John was waiting outside. He seemed relieved to see her. He had already turned the bike around when Amy hopped on the back. He hadn't pedaled two yards before the old red bicycle rose into the air. "My dad said it was real important to get the boxes back," Amy shouted over John's shoulder. He nodded. He took the old bike higher, turned and headed for Bicycle Hills.

PRISONER!

· · · · · · · · ·

16

Flying the short distance to Bicycle Hills only took a few moments. But getting in would be another matter. "Susan and Daniel are supposed to be here to help," John said as they approached the walls.

Amy looked at her watch. It was 7:35. The final game should have just started. "We need to hurry, if I'm to catch up with the club," Amy said. "Once they get very far into the Cobramaze, it can be real hard to find them."

John nodded. He turned the handlebars so the old red bike circled back toward the ominous walls of Bicycle Hills. Bright lights on tall poles shone down onto the field. "Hang on!"

John stood up on the pedals of the old red bicycle and dove down out of the sky like a dive bomber. Just before he was about to pass over the walls, he hit the lever on the light switch. The instant the light came on, the walls around Bicycle Hills started to shoot up like giant dark bricks. But the light of the bike pierced a hole in the darkness. And through that hole shot the old bicycle with the two riders. As soon as they were on the other side, a bell began to ring loudly over the field like a burglar alarm. The bike wavered and seemed to lose power. John struggled to keep it up in the air.

"Something's wrong," he yelled. The bike dipped suddenly, almost crashing into one of the small hills. John jerked the handlebars to the side missing another hill. Then the bike hit the ground hard. Amy held on tightly to John's waist. Then the bike stopped.

The bell kept ringing. That's when a small hill right in front of them about five feet high began to break open as if it were an eggshell. Suddenly two red glowing lights shone out of the crack. Then Amy realized they were the eyes of some strange creature that looked like the ones Amy had seen in the mirror back at her house. "It's one of the Daimones," John whispered.

Both children stared at the creature, too surprised and afraid to move. Then other hills around them began to screech and crack open. More sets of the red eyes appeared and moved slowly forward.

"Run for it!" John yelled. Amy jumped off the Spirit Flyer.

"What about you?" Amy asked. The creatures were walking toward John.

"Go get your friends!" John yelled again. "I'll get help."

Amy ran toward the center hill. When she reached the door, she looked back. John appeared to be surrounded by even more of the strange creatures. They stretched out their hands toward John. Amy took a last look at her friend and then stuck her hand into the dark oily window. She was sucked through in an instant.

Amy ran for the rainbow elevator. The big blue doors opened, and she began to descend. When she got out she realized that the games had already begun. Every available mask, uniform and weapon was gone from the rack and not a child was in sight. She heard shouts and voices. "I bet every kid in Centerville is down in the Cobramaze tonight," Amy said to herself. "They're all looking for the last big treasure to win the Final Game."

Amy started running down the dimly lit passageways. Though it had been a week since she had played the game, the passageways seemed familiar. Before running into each new room, she spied it out carefully to make sure she wouldn't be shot or captured. Without her Faster Blaster, she felt defenseless, but she was determined not to play the game anyway. Amy moved as fast as she felt was safe through the Cobramaze until she came to Nesting Den.

She was relieved when she saw all the kids in the Super Wings in the chamber. They had on their gray uniforms and the cobrahood masks. Tiffany was holding the Trag 7 box in one hand and a birdcage in the other.

She looked surprised to see Amy. "You decided to play after all." Tiffany didn't sound very happy to see her, Amy thought.

"Our prize player," Sloan said with a big grin. "I knew you wouldn't let us down. But where's your uniform and Faster Blaster? You can't play without those." The other Super Wings players surrounded Amy. They looked happy to see her.

"I came but I decided not to play," Amy said. "And I want to get the Trag 7 unit back. I gave it to you, and I want it back. Now."

"You're kidding," Tiffany said. She clutched the black box possessively. "The Trag 7 is going to help us beat that double-crossing Barry Smedlowe once and for all. He'll be lower than a Rank Blank before we get done."

"Give it to me," Amy said firmly. "Where's the other one?"

"It's safe," Sloan said. "I told you we would return them tomorrow."

"My dad said to bring them back," Amy insisted. "He said they're dangerous and top secret, and he wants me to get them back. And there's something bad about this place, especially tonight of all nights. I think we all need to leave right now. We need to warn everyone to stop playing the game. Something terrible is about to happen."

"Are you kidding?" Sloan asked. "Stop the game? What kind of spoil-sport are you? You're just spooked because it's Halloween. We'll be the winners of the game and each have our own Trag 7 before this night is over. Then it will be our turn to howl. We need the Trag 7 to win. That box is our secret weapon and no one is giving it back."

"For someone who's so smart, you can sure be a dumb chicken," Mary Ann said and laughed. "Cluck, cluck, cluck!" The other kids laughed at Mary Ann's chicken sounds. Amy tried to ignore the remarks, but she felt her face getting red.

"Let's go," Tiffany said. "We need to get to the Cobra Den ahead of Barry so we can use the Trag 7."

"Yeah," the other kids said.

"I want that box," Amy said. And in a quick motion, she grabbed it away from a surprised Tiffany. Amy started to run. Tiffany lunged toward Amy, but she was off balance because she was holding the birdcage. The cage dropped to the ground.

"The bird!" Sloan yelled. But the cage door fell open and the little sparrow flew out. Everyone grabbed for the bird, but it flew high above their outstretched hands and disappeared down a dark passageway. Tiffany tackled Amy and they both fell. The Trag 7 bounced out of Amy's hands. Sloan ran over and picked up the mysterious black box. He glared at Amy.

"You lost the bird," he spat out at Amy. "Do you know how hard it is to catch a wild bird? And we don't have time to catch another one."

Amy jumped up and reached for the box, but the other kids in the club grabbed her arms. Amy yanked and pulled, but they were too strong.

"Take her prisoner," Sloan said. The older boy looked furious. "Use our best ropes. She's a traitor to the club."

Amy jerked her arms as Tiffany pulled the ropes out of her backpack. In moments, Amy's arms were pinned to her sides. Her hands were free, but seemed useless. "Let me go!" Amy yelled. "Let me . . ." A gray gag-rag slipped around her mouth and was yanked tight. Amy screamed, but her words were swallowed by the rag.

"We'll have to take her with us, otherwise she might try to spoil the game somehow," Sloan said with cool determination.

"But what will we do for a sacrifice?" Tiffany asked. "The box was supposed to use the blood of a wild bird."

Everyone looked to Sloan. He stared at the black box, thinking. He took out his C & C Rules manual from his backpack. Then he turned to the secret manual on the Trag 7. He looked through the pages quickly. He read a page. Then he looked up.

"We won't be without blood," Sloan said with a hard grin. "After all, we have our prisoner here. She's lost the bird, so she'll be the one to pay. We'll have our blood, and we'll have our sacrifice. The blood of a traitor will work."

"Is that in the rules?" Tiffany asked.

"Not exactly," Sloan said. "But surely the blood of a person is just as good as a stupid bird." The other children looked at each other with wild excited eyes. Amy jerked on the ropes, but her hands were held tight. "Don't worry, Amy," Sloan said. "It's only a game. We'll only take a few drops of blood. The rules say that should be enough. When the game is over tonight, we'll let the Big Board decide your fate, since you've become a traitor."

The hooded heads of the twenty Super Wings nodded with agreement. The club formed a circle and crossed their arms and held hands. They hissed and then cheered.

"Now let's get back those points and win the game," Sloan said firmly. "We've got some treasure to win." He looked at his map, then headed down a tunnel. The other C & C commandos followed. Two of the boys took Amy by the arms while Tiffany grabbed the ropes. They pulled their prisoner into the tunnel.

THE
BOMB
· · · · · · · ·
17

Amy stopped struggling as the guards of the
Super Wings Club dragged her deeper and deeper into the Cobramaze
below Bicycle Hills. She walked along, trying to think of a way to get
the Trag 7 and escape. The others seemed more excited than usual.
Maybe it was because it was the Final Game, or maybe it was because
of Halloween. Amy felt deep inside herself that there was something
different about this night of all nights, and it wasn't good.

Sloan had deciphered a code which showed a secret passageway
through the Cobramaze. There was only one known entrance into the
Cobra Master's Den and that was on all the maps. Sloan had spent a lot

of the golden point tokens to buy this special map from Uncle Bunkie. The secret passageway, called the Vanishing Tunnel, led to the Cobra Master's Den, and no one, the clown said, would know about it. The secret passageway also helped them avoid being seen by other clubs. Normally, the Super Wings liked to have encounters and combat with other clubs. Shooting the Faster Blasters and taking the spoils of war was one of the best things about playing C & C. But since they had been ambushed by Barry and his club, they couldn't risk losing any more players or points.

Time was critical if Sloan's plan was to work. The Super Wings had to be the first ones to find the Cobra's Den. He had a plan for how to use the Trag 7 in the most effective way. But without the bird, he wasn't sure if the plan would work. Still there was nothing else to do but press on.

Moving down the secret Vanishing Tunnel was difficult, especially since it was so narrow. It was especially hard for Amy. More than once she fell down and was dragged along the dusty floor before she got back to her feet. Amy moaned into the gag, but no one was listening.

It seemed like they had been walking a long time in the dimly lit passageway before everyone had to get down on their knees and crawl through a hole. "Are you sure this is the right way?" Mary Ann grumbled at one particularly narrow place.

"Of course this is the right way," Sloan hissed. He was about to say more when he saw an opening ahead. He held up his arm, motioning for everyone to keep quiet. Sloan crept forward slowly to the mouth of the opening. He crawled out of sight and then reappeared. He smiled and waved the others forward. "We're here," Sloan said. "We made it to the Cobra's Den."

The kids crowded into the opening. A large boulder covered up the mouth of the secret tunnel. But as they peeked out from behind the rock, they saw the largest room they had ever seen in the Cobramaze. It was as big as the gymnasium at school. Right in the center was a tremendously large statue of a giant cobra, coiled, with its head raised up in the air, looking like it was ready to strike. The mouth was open and the long fangs were bared. Amy stared at the huge snake and began to feel afraid.

"Wow!" whispered Tiffany. "That cobra must be fifty feet high."

"It's bigger than that," Sloan said. "Look! Down below him. There's the treasure chest. Look at the size of that thing." The other children stared with their mouths open. The old wooden chest seemed to be as big as the back of a pickup truck. The lid was closed. A large heavy padlock guarded the unknown contents.

"How will we open it?" Tiffany asked.

"And how will we carry it all out?" Mary Ann added.

"We'll find a way," Sloan said. "Once we win, we'll have the others as our prisoners. We'll make them carry it for us."

"I can't wait to see that sneaky Barry carrying my treasure for me as my slave," Tiffany said.

The kids scrambled down the crude stone steps that led into the Cobra's Den. Large egg-shaped boulders almost six feet high lay scattered over the floor of the cavern.

"There's only one other passageway that leads into this place," Sloan said, looking carefully around the room. "And no one can see the Vanishing Tunnel."

"Let's go see the treasure," Mary Ann said. "I can't wait."

"That's not the plan," Sloan said firmly. "We're going to do this my way. We could maybe get the treasure now, but I want revenge. I want to take Smedlowe prisoner, personally. Even if we took the treasure, we'd still have to get back out. The other commandos might discover the Vanishing Tunnel once they get here. I don't want to risk it. We could be ambushed. With my plan, we'll get the treasure, kill points and all the points and tokens of everyone. We'll let everyone arrive and fight it out for the treasure. Then when they think they got it made, we use our secret weapon. That's what you do in a war." Sloan held up the Trag

7 unit so everyone could see. "With a few drops of blood, this thing will become a bomb," Sloan said. "With the blood, the Trag 7 becomes what you wish it to be, the manual says. And I want it to be a bomb. We'll bomb 'em all."

"Blast them to smithereens!" Tiffany shouted.

"Nuke 'em into the next county!" shouted someone else.

Everyone laughed nervously.

"Then after the bomb goes off, we'll go down and clean up," Sloan said. "We'll have all the treasure, all the prisoners, all the points. Everything. We'll be so far ahead in points that we'll be the rulers of Bicycle Hills for the rest of this year and maybe forever!"

Everyone cheered except Amy, who kept squirming, hoping somehow to loosen the ropes. Sloan patted the Trag 7 box. The others grinned excitedly. Amy shook her head from side to side and tried to warn them, but no one was paying any attention.

That's when they heard voices. The Super Wings scrambled back up the stone steps, and went back into the Vanishing Tunnel. Within moments, two other hooded commandos appeared. By the armband insignia they could tell they were the members of the Cobra Club. They entered the large room cautiously, with their Faster Blasters raised, ready to shoot. Then five more members of the Cobra Club entered through the tunnel. They had their Blasters ready. They ran quickly around the room, searching behind large egg-shaped boulders scattered around the cavern floor. One of the Cobra Club members looked in the direction of the Vanishing Tunnel, but didn't see anything suspicious.

When the scouts seemed satisfied that the Cobra Den was empty, they waved their hands. That's when the prisoners started coming in. Sloan and the others in the club were amazed. The prisoners kept coming and coming. It seemed like half the kids in town had been taken prisoner by the Cobra Club.

"How could he have done it?" Scott asked Sloan in a whisper.

"Who knows?" Sloan replied. "He must have tricked them somehow."

Then Barry appeared with a big smile on his face. With him were members of each of the prisoner clubs. "He did trick them," Sloan whimpered. "He must have gotten one person in each club to betray their club. That guy is really an operator."

The rest of the Cobra Club marched in. They scattered around the room, their Faster Blasters ready, watching the entrance to the tunnel.

"We made it," Barry said loudly, looking up at the giant stone cobra that appeared ready to strike. "And all we have to do is wait for those stupid Super Wings to get here. Then we'll blast them and take home the treasure."

"Cheater," one of the prisoners yelled out.

"Don't be a spoilsport," Barry said, then laughed his awful braying laugh. "Treason is the name of the game. You were betrayed and ambushed fair and square."

"I still say it's cheating," another prisoner grumbled.

"Let's divide the treasure like you promised," said Richard Nichols, the betrayer of the Snake-eyes Club. "You said we would divide it."

"Yeah," said the others in the group who had betrayed their own clubs.

"A deal's a deal," Barry said with a smile. "You guys get up to half the treasure to divide among yourselves, and the Cobra Club gets the other half."

"But we get first pick, right?" said Melissa Jackson, the betrayer of the Blaster Club. "That's what you said."

"That's the deal," Barry said. "But you better hurry before the others get here."

All the betrayers, young and old, ran for the treasure chest. There were almost twenty of them gathered around, trying to figure a way to unlock the box. Sloan waited and watched. The other members of the Cobra Club raised their weapons.

"I got the lock open," one of the boys yelled excitedly. The others began to lift the lid of the large wooden chest.

"Now!" Barry yelled. The Cobra Club let loose their fire. The air was filled with Glitter Globs which rained down like hail on the greedy betrayers. All together in one place, they were an easy target. Within a minute, each one had been hit at least twice.

"You're captured!" Barry yelled triumphantly. "Now the treasure is all ours and ours alone."

"Cheater!" one of the boys yelled out, trying to wipe off the glitter glob. "You can't shoot us."

"Of course I can, you idiot," Barry said. "You didn't really think I would let you clowns have half the treasure, did you?"

"Serves you right," grunted the leader of the Snake-eyes Club to Richard. "You betrayed us and he betrayed you."

"Everyone is a prisoner except our club," Barry said proudly. "And there's no way Sloan can get to the treasure with the tunnel under guard. He has to come to us, and we'll be waiting. So let's just have a look at that treasure while we wait."

The Cobra Club members moved toward the treasure chest. Barry climbed up on one of the large egg-shaped boulders and smiled down at all the kids who had been taken prisoner. There must have been over three hundred C & C commandos crowded beneath the stony gaze of the giant Cobra statue.

"Let's do it now," Sloan whispered to Scott. "Get Amy."

The two guards dragged Amy to the mouth of the Vanishing Tunnel. Tiffany took the Trag 7 box while Sloan opened his pack. He pulled out a long shiny needle. Amy struggled harder when she saw it.

"If you hadn't lost our bird, you wouldn't be in this position," Sloan whispered harshly.

"Maybe we should just use our Faster Blasters," Scott said nervously as he looked at the needle. "We don't really know what that box will do. We could take them with the Blasters. There's less than twenty Cobra Club members."

The leader of the Super Wings shook his hooded head. A distant look

was in his eye. "I want to use the bomb," Sloan said. "I'll bomb them all. That'll show everyone who's got the most power in this stupid little town. I'll show Smedlowe he can't mess with me and get away with it."

The entire club gathered at the mouth of the tunnel to watch. With one quick motion, Sloan grabbed Amy's hand and jabbed her thumb with the needle. The prick hurt, but that wasn't what frightened Amy. It was the box. It seemed like something was moving inside it. The other kids stared with wild eyes at the little ball of blood on Amy's thumb. Then everything seemed to happen at once. Sloan pushed her thumb onto the box. The instant the blood touched the dark surface, a sound like distant thunder rumbled through the room. The floor of the room began to shake. The Trag 7 began to flicker deep inside, as if it were filled with flashes of blue lightning. Sloan stared at the box as if hypnotized.

"Throw it!" Tiffany shouted.

Down below, everyone had stood still as the sound of the thunder and the rumbling earth caught their attention. Sloan stood up and walked from behind the large boulder. "Death to all!" Sloan yelled out. Every kid in the room looked up at the leader of the Super Wings Club. Sloan then hurled the flashing box down at them. The box flew out in the air. But instead of falling, it floated right up in front of the statue of the large stone Cobra.

"Let's get out of here," Tiffany yelled. The others turned to run back inside the Vanishing Tunnel. That's when the rumbling increased and a great cracking noise split the air right behind the Super Wings Club. The rocks above the mouth of the Vanishing Tunnel suddenly broke apart and crashed down in a heap of rubble and dust. The Vanishing Tunnel had vanished in front of their eyes.

"We're trapped!" Tiffany screamed.

"The other tunnel," Sloan yelled. The Super Wings started down the stone steps, leaving Amy behind. But it was too late. In a whoosh and a crack, the Trag 7 exploded in a blast of sparkle and blue fire.

THE
COBRA

· · · · · · · · ·

18

The air was filled with a sparkling orange fog of light that was so thick it was hard to breathe. The sparkles had filled the room, covering everyone with a fine spray of glitter. The children who had been knocked over by the blast slowly got up, slapping their uniforms, trying to dust off the glitter. Amy raised her head slowly. Her ropes had been loosened during the blast. She struggled with her hands and arms to get them off.

"You're dead!" Sloan yelled out as he climbed up on one of the egg-shaped boulders. "We bombed you all."

"You didn't win," Barry said, slapping the glitter out of his uniform.

"You blew yourselves up too. Your whole team is covered with glitter. Your club is just as dead as our club."

Sloan started to argue, but realized that what Barry said was true. By the rules of the game, since they were just as covered with the glitter, they were considered hit. The members of the Super Wings Club got off the floor of the cave and glared at Sloan.

"I told you to use our Blasters," Scott said. "We're all dead. Now no one wins the Final Game."

"Get the treasure!" Barry yelled. Everyone moved toward the large chest in a sudden free-for-all. Those closest knocked open the lid and reached inside. They stopped at what they saw. Richard Nichols, the betrayer of the Snake-eyes Club, reached down and pulled out a handful of gray dust. He poured it slowly back into the large chest.

"What is it?" Sloan asked, fighting his way through the crowd to the treasure chest. "I claim it in the name of the Super Wings Club since we were the last ones officially alive. Besides, I set off the bomb."

"You can have it," Richard said with disgust. "It's ashes. Nothing but ashes."

"Ashes?" Sloan said. He stared at the gray powder pouring out of the older boy's hand. "It can't be ashes."

The kids crowded around the box began to murmur. Some of them cursed in disgust.

"We fought for ashes?" someone said.

"The game is over," Sloan said sadly.

"And no one is the winner?" Barry asked. He wiped some of the orange glitter off his face. "That can't be. We can't all be dead. Someone has to win."

"The game indeed is over," the voice of Uncle Bunkie announced. Everyone turned toward the tunnels. Uncle Bunkie had appeared without anyone noticing. His big red smile seemed bigger than usual. He stared with great satisfaction at the crowd of children, their C & C commando uniforms covered with the orange sticky glitter.

"But who won?" Sloan demanded.

"What do the dead ever win?" the big clown asked. Then he began to laugh. "You've found the treasure chest. What does it contain? The game is over, but you won. You've all imagined well and become what you've pretended. Now the game doesn't have to end, but can go on forever and ever, just like you wanted deep inside your little dead hearts. Being dead is such a simple process. You'll get used to it. After all, you're such clever little ash eaters."

The children looked at the tall clown with confused eyes, trying to understand his strange words. They began to talk among themselves. "I don't like it down here," said one of the younger players, a third-grader named Stevie. "I want to go home."

"I wonder what time it's getting to be?" someone asked.

At the edge of the crowd, Amy struggled with her ropes. She was sure the cords were finally coming loose.

"I am going home," Richard Nichols said in disgust. He stepped back from the huge treasure chest and began to pull off the scaly hooded mask. A surprised look came over his face when the hood appeared to be stuck. He yanked hard and then yelped in pain.

"What's with you?" Sloan asked.

"The hood, I can't get it off," Richard said. "It's like it's stuck to my skin."

Some of the children gathered round. One of the girls in the Snake-eyes Club reached up to help him pull off the hood. But as soon as she touched the hood, she screamed.

"It's real," she said. "The scales feel like they're a real snake. It feels awful and creepy, just like a snakeskin."

The other kids stepped away from Richard. Richard struggled harder with the hood. Sloan pushed his way through the crowd.

"It does look real," Sloan said. He touched the scales on the back of Richard's neck. He drew back his hand quickly, as if he'd touched something very hot.

A girl in the crowd of children tried to pull off her hood, but discovered she couldn't. She screamed. "It feels like a snake," she yelled.

Amy stopped struggling with her chains and watched in amazement. Each of the children tried to pull off their C & C commando hoods, but no one succeeded. The scaly costumes not only seemed stuck to their bodies but seemed to have become a part of their person. Amy's body tensed as she watched them struggling.

"I can't get it off," Tiffany screamed. "I can't get it off."

The room filled with screams and cries as the children realized that their costumes had become part of them, or they had become part of their costumes.

"Make it stop!" an older boy yelled out. His body swayed and squirmed like a human snake.

At the mouth of the tunnel, Uncle Bunkie watched the frantic children with his big red grin. "You all win," his voice boomed out. The children stopped for a moment to listen.

"How do we get these off?" Sloan demanded. His voice cracked. "I've had enough of this game."

"Yeah," others voices added. They stared at the big clown, their eyes full of fear.

"This is your special Halloween treat," Uncle Bunkie announced. "Soon your transformation will be complete. As I said earlier, the game is only beginning. You didn't want to be bored, and you won't be bored with death, I assure you. Each of you has won and reached your deepest potential. You have been born of the serpent, so naturally, you look like him. Halloween is a night when your true natures can be seen." The big clown pointed up to the great stone statue of the gigantic cobra. "There is your father and mother," he said. "Have fun."

Uncle Bunkie laughed, then turned his back on the children and disappeared into the tunnel. For a while, the children heard his laughter echoing down into the great room. Then they heard nothing but silence.

"Wait!" Sloan yelled. "How do we get these things . . ."

A sudden crack split the air, as if lightning had filled the cavern.

"Look!" a girl named Sharon yelled. She pointed at the statue of the giant coiled cobra. Right above the eyes, the stone had cracked. The children stared at the giant serpent. Another crack appeared near the opened mouth. The statue almost seemed to move. Then suddenly, another crack appeared and a piece of stone fell off, like the shell of an egg. The falling stone hit the floor and broke into a thousand pieces. The crowd of children quickly moved back as another piece of rock fell off the statue. The floor of the cavern began to rumble and groan. All eyes were on the serpent as another piece of rock fell and then another. Below the shell of rock was a great quivering darkness. More and more of the stone fell off as if the serpent were shedding its skin of stone. Huge plates of rock fell off the serpent's eyes.

Amy suddenly knew what she would see. The ropes finally came loose and she ripped the gag off her mouth. "It's more than a statue!" Amy yelled. But no sooner were the words were out of her mouth than the huge eyes began to glow red. The crowd of children gasped. Then the head of the great serpent moved. The red eyes looked blankly down on the children, then the great mouth opened and a loud hiss filled the room as the great fangs glistened, wet with poison.

The cavern was filled with screams. The children in the commando uniforms stampeded for the tunnel that led out of the Cobra's Den. Amy was knocked down in the sudden rush. She thought she would be trampled for sure.

The giant snake began to sway back and forth, shrugging off the great pieces of stone. The plates of rock fell like huge scales. Amy struggled to her feet. Most of the children were in the tunnel, running. Somebody jerked Amy by her arm, pulling her up. Soon she was running with the rest of them. She ran into the mouth of the tunnel, not daring to look back.

The cavern was empty except for the giant cobra, which continued to sway back and forth, breaking the stone barrier. Soon the entire body was free. The great serpent rose up, spreading its hood. The mouth opened with a hiss that roared so loud the walls of the Cobra Den shook. The red eyes seemed to be on fire as they looked for the children. Then the snake lowered itself. The head entered the tunnel as the long body began to uncoil. The cobra barely fit into the passageway, its scales scraping against the rock. The reptile slithered slowly into the darkness, following the scent of fear and the echoing screams of the children.

OUT OF THE
SERPENT'S
MOUTH
• • • • • • • • •

19

Amy was at the end of the long trail of running children. The tunnel was filled more with the sound of running footsteps than screams. Most children quickly discovered it was difficult to run and scream at the same time for very long. All they wanted was to escape, to be the first ones up the rainbow-colored elevator. Amy shared those same thoughts—escape before it was too late. But deep inside, she didn't think they would make it. The whole Halloween night had been too strange and things only seemed to be getting worse.

For a while the kids in the permanent costumes seemed to be running upward, toward the surface of the earth. But then the tunnel curved slowly and they seemed to be going downward. Amy thought she heard noises in the tunnel behind her, but she was too afraid to look back. She just kept running, following the others before her.

She was relieved when up ahead she saw the tunnel widening. She was right on the heels of those ahead of her when they ran out into a large cavernous room. Amy was surprised to see Sloan and Tiffany and all the other children stopped, looking anxiously around the room. Amy looked up. Then she realized the same thing the other children knew— they were all back in the gigantic Cobra's Den again. The huge treasure chest of ashes was in the center. Large egg-shaped boulders lay scattered around the room. The tunnel had taken them in a long circle.

"The tunnel changed somehow," Barry Smedlowe said to Sloan. "We're back where we started. But how can that be?"

"You mean there's no way out of here?" Tiffany asked, saying out loud what all the other children were thinking. All eyes turned to where the statue of the giant cobra had been. All that remained was a heap of stones that looked like large stone scales. One of the younger children began to cry as he realized what that meant. But his cries were drowned out by the sound of a roaring hiss, coming out of the tunnel. The children ran for the opposite wall away from the tunnel. Their screams were drowned out by another hiss, which seemed even louder. Amy, like the others, flattened herself against the wall and stared at the mouth of the tunnel. A red glow appeared out of the darkness and slowly grew brighter and brighter.

Then the blunt head of the giant cobra appeared. The harsh red eyes stared blankly at the hundreds of children. The cobra flicked out its wet tongue and slowly slithered into its den. The great black body seemed to ooze out of the tunnel on and on like a river of flowing darkness. The serpent rose into the air as it moved into the room. It spread its hood. The white circled X on its throat almost seemed to quiver. The snake seemed even larger than before even though half its body was still in the tunnel.

The children stared at the cobra. No one moved. The snake opened its great mouth. The wet fangs arched downward. With a sudden snap of the great head, a flash of blue electric light shot out of the snake's mouth. The children's screams were drowned out by the roar as loud as thunder.

Amy screamed too, blinded by the flash of light. She wasn't sure how long the blindness lasted but during that time she felt a tingling electric feeling from head to toe. When the tingling left, the cavern slowly came back into view. Then came a sense of great heaviness. Amy recognized the familiar bad feeling right away. She looked down and saw what she knew would be there and had been there all along—the great dark chain. The entire room seemed to shimmer in an eerie glow of blue light, and each child wore a chain locked with a neck ring.

For a moment, the room was filled with new murmurs and noise as the children forgot about the great snake and concentrated on their chains. "What does it mean?" a girl sobbed. Her hands touched the cold links. Some children tried to pull the chains off. Others tried removing their Cobrahoods again. But both the chains and the scaly snake hoods seemed to be just as much a part of them as their ears or fingers. The room was filled with dull clinking sounds and moans as child after child tried to pull off the heavy dark chains.

"I wanna go home," a little boy wailed in the twilight. "I wanna go home." But the long Halloween night continued on.

Amy looked at the other children struggling and remembered the images she had seen in the cracked mirror on John Kramar's old red bike. It seemed like a long time since he had flown over the walls of Bicycle Hills. She wondered what had happened to him. But she was startled out of her thoughts when the giant snake hissed again, the eyes glowing fire red.

The children struggling with their chains stopped to watch the great serpent. Without a sound, the head began to drop lower and lower. The children tried to press themselves into the rock. Finally, the opened mouth of the serpent rested on the floor of the cavern. The fiery red eyes of the snake stared out at the captive audience.

"Look," Sloan whispered. He pointed at the mouth of the serpent. Something was coming out of the mouth. Two smaller red dots appeared in the darkness of the snake's mouth. As the two lights moved forward, a figure came into view. It was the figure of a person. The figure walked stiffly. It appeared to wear the gray Caves and Cobras commando uniform. But the face seemed stiff and hard like a mask. Instead of eyes, there were two red glowing lights. And in his arms was a black square box about seven inches square—a Trag 7 unit.

"It looks like Sloan," Tiffany said in surprise. The other children began to murmur. The figure did seem to have the face of Sloan, but the body was taller, taller even than a man. Yet the face was a mask. The smiling expression seemed like a cold photograph.

"What is it?" Mary Ann asked. The figure kept walking closer and closer toward the crowd of children. Then it stopped. The red eyes of the Sloan figure seemed to be staring right at Sloan. Sloan stared back at his counterpart, looking first at the eyes, then at the Trag 7 unit in the figure's hands.

Just then, more red lights appeared in the dark mouth of the snake. More of the figures appeared, their arms outstretched, holding what appeared to be Trag 7 units. Each of them had the same gray uniform and each of them had a mask for a face. Each mask looked like someone in the room. But the glowing red eyes all looked the same.

The children were too scared to move or speak. As more of the creatures came into the room, the one with Sloan's face stood before Sloan. He lifted up the box so the boy could see. "Sloan Favor," the figure said in a voice that sounded just like Sloan. "You, as the Number One commando in Centerville, will be the first to receive your reward."

"What?" Sloan asked in surprise.

Like everyone else in the big room, Amy watched the two Sloans talking.

"Come forward and be absorbed, then the Trag 7 will be yours," the figure said. He held up the box so everyone could see.

"Be absorbed?" Sloan asked.

"Embrace your destiny," the Sloan figure said. "Tonight is a special night, a night all over the world where permission has been granted. Come receive your deepest desire. We will celebrate together, this greatest of all nights."

"Don't do it, Sloan!" Amy suddenly burst out, surprised at herself. "That thing is evil. These creatures are called Daimones and they . . ."

"Silence!" shouted the Sloan figure, its red eyes blazing brightly at Amy. The creature then waved its arm. Out of the darkness of the snake's mouth, another creature walked quickly among the others. Amy blinked in surprise when she saw a mask of her own face on the creature.

"Don't be afraid, Amy," the creature said with her own voice. "I've come to help you. I'll give you what you really want. Your stepmother doesn't understand you. Your father has been so busy. But I can show you how to make your dad love you again. Isn't that what you want?" The creature held up a Trag 7 unit and moved forward. Amy tried to run, but only took two steps before she was jerked back. The chain around her neck was stretched tight. Then she noticed that the other end of the chain was in the right hand of the creature.

"How did you do that?" Amy stopped. A moment ago, the chain hadn't appeared to be that long.

"I'm here to watch after you," the Amy figure said. "I'll take care of you, Amy. I own your chain." The Daimone moved closer. Amy jerked back hard. The ring around her neck seemed to constrict like a steel band. The creature with her face held the chain with one gloved hand and a Trag 7 unit with the other.

"You don't need to be afraid," the Amy figure said in a soothing voice. "Watch what happens with Sloan. Then follow your leader."

A few feet away, the figure with Sloan's face was slowly reeling Sloan in like a fish on a line. He was pulling the chain attached to Sloan's neck,

link by link, and the president of the Super Wings Club didn't seem to be resisting. "It will only take a short while to be absorbed," the figure with Sloan's face said. "Then all your dreams will come true. You'll have a Trag 7. Just think of the power."

Sloan looked at the box and licked his lips. Suddenly, it was as if none of the night's strange events mattered anymore. All he focused on was the box. He began to walk eagerly toward the outstretched arms of the one who bore his face.

THE KEY
AND THE
KINGDOM
• • • • • • • •

20

"Let the absorption begin!" the figure with Sloan's face cried out. The Trag 7 was laid near Sloan's feet. Sloan took a step forward as if he was in a trance. Then the figure with his face grabbed him. The eyes burned bright. Sloan screamed as if in great pain. He wiggled to get free, but the Daimone held on tight. Two older kids, a boy and a girl Amy didn't know, also went for the boxes. They began to scream as they walked into the arms of the Daimones.

The children in the room moved back at the sight. The army of the dead marched after them. A sudden wave of panic burst out all over the room. The children tried to run away, but each one was held by a chain.

Each child was matched with one of the Daimones with his or her face. The Daimones held on tightly to the dark chains and began pulling the captive children closer. Amy fought like a young horse as the Daimone with her face pulled her chain. But no matter how hard she struggled, the creature holding the other end of her chain moved closer and closer.

"Oh, help me," Amy moaned out in desperation.

"I shall help you, child," the masked figure said. "Accept the Order of the Chain and you will be free."

Amy jerked back as a reply and several feet of chain slipped through her captor's fingers. The creature roared out in a voice like a lion's growl. That's when Amy remembered the key. She quickly put her right hand in her jeans pocket. The key was there. And the instant she touched it, she knew what to do. Somehow she felt as if she had known all along. Ever since she had first seen that glimpse of the kingdom, she knew she'd had a choice to make, but she had tried to forget it. She knew her life would be changed forever if she used the key. But now she was ready. Just touching the key restored her hope. She pulled the key out of her pocket. The Daimone with her face stumbled and tripped at the sight of the kings' gift.

The heavy golden key seemed to hold its own glory and light. Just seeing the Three Crowns linked together calmed the girl. She dropped to her knees, and bowed forward until her face touched the ground. Both sorrow and joy filled her. She lifted her face with tears streaming down.

"Not that!" the creature with her face said. It lunged toward Amy as if to snatch the key out of her hand. But Amy didn't hesitate as she had once before. With a deep determination she had never known before, she slipped the key into the lock on her neck. Before she had a chance to turn it, the lock broke apart and fell off. Amy took the heavy chain, and flung it at the creature with her masked face. The Daimone with her face shrieked out, then stumbled over. The creature began to writhe and squirm and smoke and hiss.

The panic continued in the room. Hundreds of children were struggling with the Daimones. Amy looked at the key in her hand. Her first thought was to run to the next child and use the key. But she could see that the others would be overcome before she could get to them. The children, especially the little ones, were quickly tiring in their struggles

"Prince of Kings, help us all," Amy shouted out.

The words were hardly out of her mouth before a crack of light broke through the top of the room. The whole place began to shake. Amy looked up to see. The crack widened at first and then suddenly a whole section of the stone ceiling seemed to melt away as she watched. Amy wasn't the only one watching. The giant serpent suddenly rose up into the air. With a loud hiss it spread its hood. All the Daimones paused to stare.

The shaft of light continued to pour into the room, making the hole wider. Then in a flash, several red bicycles dove down into the room. The giant serpent struck, the great mouth open, the fangs ready. But the bikes were quicker. They seemed to jump to the side, just out of reach of the fangs.

Amy jumped up and down, holding the key up for John Kramar to see. The bicycle riders passed over the crowd of children. The giant cobra reared up, the red eyes blazing, waiting to strike again. The Daimones watched.

"Help us," Amy cried.

John Kramar circled around high above all the children. Then he swooped down and stopped, two feet off the ground, next to Amy.

"Climb on," John said with an easy smile.

"But what about the others?" Amy asked. The Daimones began frantically pulling the chains. The room was filled with screams once more. "There's not enough bikes."

"We didn't come alone," John said with a smile. "Look."

He pointed up toward the shaft of light pouring through the ceiling of the Cobra's Den. The light seemed rich and full and alive. Just looking at it made Amy's heart leap. But then she realized that the light was more than light. There was something in the light. Amy's mouth dropped open. There were the most beautiful creatures she had ever seen— hundreds of them, even thousands perhaps. They seemed to swim out of the light and float in the air like the wind.

"Are those the kings?" Amy asked in awe.

"Oh, no," John said. "Those are Aggeloi, the hosts and servants to the kings. And they're here to do his bidding."

The giant cobra hissed and reared back, but the air around the dark serpent was suddenly filled with a cloud of the Aggeloi. Amy blinked in surprise when she saw the great swords of light in their hands.

"You don't want to mess with the Aggeloi," John said with respect. The darkness of the giant serpent was quickly overcome with the fighting warriors of light. Though it raged, the creature quickly backed down. In a loud hiss and the red eyes blazing, the snake struck down and hit the stone floor of the room and opened a great hole. The snake seemed to drill itself downward. The rest of its long sleek body poured into the hole like a giant slithering worm. Half the army of light followed the serpent's tail into the dark pit, their swords raised.

The other half remained. As if on command, they swooped down, placing themselves between the children and the tormenting Daimones. There must have been three or four Aggeloi to every child, Amy figured. While one Aggeloi gathered a child up in his arms, the others advanced toward the Daimone, their swords drawn. The stiff gray dead creatures howled as the battle began.

The Aggeloi floated up toward the shaft of light, the children in their winglike arms. Amy could hardly believe the wonder of such a sight. They flew up out into the light, one by one, carrying the children away from the danger. Some children rode out as passengers on the old red Spirit Flyers.

Susan Kramar and Daniel Bayley had landed by Sloan and his Daimone. The creature had Sloan by the throat and was holding him in a bear hug. Both Susan and Daniel had the lights on their old Spirit Flyers aimed at Sloan. That's when a group of Aggeloi moved in to fight for the boy. Amy stared. Sloan seemed to be like a piece of rope in the middle of a tug of war. The Daimone had partially absorbed the boy, and they seemed melted together.

"Let him be free," Amy whispered as she watched them struggling. Sloan opened his eyes and looked at the Aggelois' hands. He seemed to nod, though he looked very weak. At that instant, Sloan suddenly seemed to pop loose. He fell limply into the arms of his rescuers. The boy seemed unconscious as one of the Aggeloi took him in his arms and floated up toward the shaft of light. The Daimone with Sloan's face shrieked when he saw his possession was gone. But the creature didn't have time to mourn his loss long because the Aggeloi who had fought for Sloan raised their swords and moved in, covering the dark creature with their light.

As soon as Sloan was free, Susan and Daniel aimed the lights of the old bicycles on the older boy and girl who were in the arms of the Daimones. Both of their bodies were jerking and twitching as if electricity was shocking them. Though the Aggeloi tried pulling them free, these children were held tight.

"I want the Trag 7," the older boy chattered. "Leave me alone."

With those words, the Aggeloi let go of him. In an instant, the Daimone and the boy seemed to melt into one person. The same thing happened with the older girl. She and the Daimone with her face, suddenly just seemed to merge before Susan and Daniel's eyes. The Aggeloi left her. There was nothing else to be done.

The hole the giant serpent escaped down was cracking and widening by the second as more and more stones and rocks fell in it. Then the walls of the room began to crack and crumble. Great slabs of stone fell and disappeared down the hole.

"Let's get out of here," John said. "We've gotten what we came for." Susan, Daniel and the other Spirit Flyer bike riders were already headed up in the air. Amy held tightly onto John's waist as they joined the others. Amy smiled when she saw four of the beautiful Aggeloi floating along next to each of the old bicycles. She looked over her shoulder at the Aggeloi still fighting. Then she and John entered the shaft of light.

The whole world seemed to have fallen away once they entered the light. She felt as if she was flowing in a river of music and wonder. And up ahead, she saw a beautiful green place, a place brighter than day.

"This is the kingdom again, isn't it?" Amy asked.

"This is part of it," John said with a nod. The bike coasted to a stop. They were in the midst of all the Aggeloi and children. The children still wore their chains, but their eyes were open. Some of them were holding golden keys and looking at the locks.

"It looks better without that chain hanging around my neck," Amy said.

"Everything is better without those chains," John replied and turned and winked. "I'm glad you used that key when you did. I'm not sure we could have broken through in time. The darkness in the air tonight is like none we've ever seen before. Ever since I dropped you off we've been battling the forces of the air. The Daimones seemed to be swarming as thick as mosquitoes."

"There sure were a lot of them underneath the ground too," Amy said.

The children were hovering above Bicycle Hills. Amy looked at the dark hills. A rumble came and the hills shook. "An earthquake," John said. The ground of Bicycle Hills seemed to be in torment. The earth churned and broke apart in wide cracks. And the center hill, the entrance to the world below, opened up into a hole. Suddenly the whole field seemed to buckle and fall in. The hole in the center grew as the rest of the field fell in on itself.

Then there was quiet.

"Did you see that?" Amy asked, looking out at the darkness from the safety of the kingdom.

"The night isn't over," John replied. He seemed relieved, but there was still a concerned look on his face Amy was about to ask him what he was worried about when a greater flash of light passed over them.

"He's here," John said simply.

Amy turned. Her eyes met the eyes of the Prince of Kings. They seemed to look through her to her core. Amy had never felt such acceptance and love. She instantly remembered the first time she had really seen him. He had seemed sadder at that first visit because the chain had held her back from entering fully into his presence. There had been such a strange kind of longing in his eyes then. But now there was freedom. Amy smiled and he smiled back.

"He's really something, isn't he?" Amy burst out, turning toward John.

The boy on the bicycle nodded. For a moment, Amy lost all sense of time, watching the Prince of Kings show himself to the other children. One by one, he visited each of them. She could tell that they too were discovering the dark invisible chains that only became visible in the realm of the Deeper World and the light of the kingdom.

"I only wish the kingdom would come and stay," John said, a little sad. "The kingdom is here for a while, it seems, but not like it will be one day."

Then as he had come, the Prince of Kings was gone. The great light slowly faded as his presence lingered. Then the Aggeloi were gone and with them their light. The kingdom had faded away from sight and the night returned.

The children found themselves on the Cemetery Road, just outside the boundaries of Bicycle Hills. They seemed to be dazed as they stood on the road, shaking their heads, trying to adjust to all the sudden changes. They seemed confused, as if waking up from a dream.

The only light left came from the lights of the distant factory, country club and town. Rapidly approaching headlights of cars came down the long drive of the country club. That's when Amy heard the distant sirens coming from the direction of town. Cars were streaming out of the club. There was mass confusion when they came to Cemetery Road. Some wanted to go toward town, others came toward Bicycle Hills as parents looked for their children. Amy thought there would be a huge traffic jam in about five minutes. Some children recognized their parents' car and flagged them down. Cars stopped as children got in. The headlights of a car stopped near Amy and the car honked. Amy saw it was her father and stepmother.

"I see my parents," Amy said to John.

"You better go," John said. He seemed a little disappointed. Something about the boy seemed uncomfortable.

"Why do you look so worried?" Amy asked. "Everyone got out in time. You helped save us all. They saw the kingdom too."

"The night isn't over," John said simply. "You haven't heard the news."

"What news?" Amy asked.

Her dad honked the car again. Then he stuck his head out of the window. "Amy, come on," he yelled. "We need to get home right away."

Her father sounded strangely urgent. Amy looked at John. Without speaking, she took a step toward him and quickly kissed his cheek.

"Thanks," Amy said with a smile. "Thanks for everything." Then she ran for the car.

THE
LONG
NIGHT

• • • • • • • •

21

Amy's father gunned the engine as soon as she got in the car. They were moving before her door was shut. "What's the rush?" Amy asked. "And why are the sirens blowing. Is there a fire?"

"Worse than that," Dr. Burke said. In the rearview mirror, Amy could see the worried expression on her father's face. "Did you get those units?"

"No," Amy said. "One sort of exploded. But most of the kids are all right. I thought for sure you'd all be gone home by now. I was down under Bicycle Hills so long."

"What do you mean?" her stepmother asked. "You just left. I was afraid you'd be lost in that field somewhere when we need to be home in the basement."

"Just left?" Amy asked. "I must have been gone for hours." Amy looked down at her watch. The digits said 7:45. Amy blinked in surprise. "It's only quarter till eight?" she asked.

"They called the party off at the country club early too," her father said. He was driving as fast as he could and was right on the bumper of the car in front of him. "Once the news came over the speakers, everyone left."

"What news?" Amy asked.

The tires on the car squealed as Dr. Burke turned a corner onto Oak Street. He gunned the engine. The sirens were loud. "You haven't heard?" her stepmother asked. "Our country is at war. And so is the whole world. Everything has just gone crazy."

Amy sat in a daze as the words sank in. The sirens were so loud in town, it was hard to think. Before she knew it, Dr. Burke pulled the car into the driveway at home. Her stepmother ran into the house carrying little Sarah in her arms. Her father took Amy's arm.

"Go to the basement," her father said as they got in the house. Her stepmother was getting baby supplies. Dr. Burke locked the front door and then ran upstairs. Amy turned on the lights at the top of the stairs, then went down in the basement and sat down on their old couch. The basement was damp and cool and quite junky. A lot of their old furniture was stored there. She sat on the couch.

Mrs. Burke carried down the baby and baby bag. Dr. Burke had the fold-up playpen. Amy felt numb as she watched them setting things up. Dr. Burke ran back up the stairs. A few minutes later he returned with a portable TV and a radio. He plugged them in. Amy could still hear the sirens wailing outside. The TV came on, but all they saw was snow. Dr. Burke quickly punched a button that went through all the other channels.

"The satellite transmitters have probably been destroyed," he said grimly. He turned on the radio. He quickly found a talking voice. It was the radio station from Unionville, a nearby town.

". . . is suggesting going to your basements or any room without windows," the voice said. "Fill your tubs and available containers with water. No one is sure how long the emergency situation will last. But a state of emergency has been declared."

Dr. Burke ran up the stairs. Amy heard water running. She turned her attention back to the radio. The announcer mostly talked about the best ways to take shelter and what other radio frequencies were operating for official government reports. After a few minutes, Dr. Burke came down the stairs. He held a plastic milk jug full of water. His face looked very tired and old, Amy thought.

"The water pressure is practically zero," he announced. "I have some in the tub. Everyone in town must be trying to collect water. I suppose we could drink water from the tank on the toilet."

"Drink water from the toilet?" Amy exclaimed. Her father looked serious.

The voice on the radio paused. "We will now try to relay the official military reports already in progress," the voice said. There was another pause. The voice came out of the radio abruptly.

". . . and attacked in response. The extent of the casualties isn't known at this time, but losses are expected to be heavy. The government requests that all persons . . ." The voice was suddenly gone, faded away into static. Amy tensed, waiting for the voice to come back on. All she heard was the electric crackling noise.

Her father waited, then turned the channels. He found voices, but suddenly the lights and radio went out. Outside, Amy heard the slow dying of the sirens. "The electricity must have gone off," her father said. The Burke family sat in the dark. Amy wrapped her arms around her shoulders. Dr. Burke flipped on a flashlight. "The batteries are old in this thing," he said in a normal tone of voice. "Let's get the sleeping situation set up while we have light."

"I wish we had a radio with a battery," Mrs. Burke said.

"Daddy, I'm scared," Amy said.

"Everyone is scared," he said. "Now help me move these couches together." Dr. Burke lay the small flashlight down on an end table. In the weak light, Amy helped her father shove the two old couches together. They put the playpen in the center. For an instant, the lights in the room flickered on and then went dark again. Dr. Burke threw some blankets on the couch.

"Let's just try to rest," he said. "I know it's still early, but we can't do any more in this darkness. We'll just wait until morning."

"If we . . ." Mrs. Burke started to speak, then stopped. Amy looked at her stepmother. She was clutching the baby to her chest and staring off into the dark part of the basement.

"Amy, get your covers and lie down," Dr. Burke said. "Then I'm going to turn off the flashlight to conserve the batteries."

Amy pulled an old heavy worn quilt up to her chin. She kicked off her sneakers. Mrs. Burke lay down with the baby still in her arms. Dr. Burke went over and sat down next to his wife. He lay down next to her. He flipped off the light. The room was plunged into darkness. She pulled the covers up tighter to her chin.

She had intended to tell her parents all about her adventures down under Bicycle Hills and the rescue by the Aggeloi and how she saw the Prince of Kings himself. Just thinking about that made her feel better. She reached into her pocket and held the golden key.

Her father talked about what they would try to do tomorrow. Then he and Mrs. Burke began whispering. Amy couldn't hear their words, but she could hear the worry in their voices. She lay huddled on the couch, wondering if tomorrow would be there for them. Like John Kramar had said, the long night wasn't over yet. Amy wondered if a new day would ever come again. And if it did, what it would mean. She wondered if John and the other kids on Spirit Flyer bikes were still out in the darkness or if they were at home with their families.

Out in the night, a dog was barking far away. Amy lay in fear for a long time, it seemed, but finally she was too tired to be scared and gave in to the night, falling into sleep, holding the golden key. In her dreams, the Prince of Kings talked to her, telling her she would be safe.

SEEKING THE KINGDOM

· · · · · · · · ·

22

The long Halloween night finally ended. The next day came and Centerville was still there. And so was most of the world, though everything had changed and shifted over the course of a single long night. There was a kind of numbness and shock those first few days.

Like most people, Amy and her stepmother stayed in the house all day Saturday and Sunday on advice of the Centerville sheriff's office and the town council. Only Dr. Burke went outside. He drove his car to the Goliath factory and around town to find out the news. The electricity came on and off. Amy gave up trying to watch TV or listen to her radio.

Instead she read a book and sat on her new bicycle.

Actually, she sat on an old bicycle. After the long Halloween night finally ended, she went upstairs the next morning to her room and was surprised to find an old red bicycle with big balloon tires leaning against her bed. Noble white letters spelled the name: *Spirit Flyer*. Amy had been extremely excited about the bicycle and had almost forgotten the situation in the rest of the world for a while.

Just sitting on the old bike seemed to bring the world into a new light. Though Amy had been afraid like never before on Halloween night, sitting on the old bike put those fears in a different perspective. More than anything, she wished she could ride the old bike. She wanted to find John Kramar and the other children with Spirit Flyer bikes. She had a million questions. Deep inside, she felt like she was on the edge of an exciting new adventure.

Though she told her parents about the appearance of the mysterious old bike, neither one quite seemed to believe her. Her father seemed more nervous and depressed than ever with the events in town and in the world. He seemed to be numbed by it all.

The electricity came back on and stayed on Monday morning. School was called off. In fact, school was called off for the whole week and maybe longer. The town and state and national elections that were to take place were also postponed. The government was in a shambles. Emergency measures and martial law had been declared across the nation.

"Can't I go out today for a little while?" Amy asked her father that morning. "I'm tired of being stuck in the house all the time." Her father seemed reluctant. He rubbed his face. Dark patches were under his eyes. He wasn't sleeping well.

"I'd like to take Sarah Jane out in the stroller myself," Mrs. Burke said. "I could talk with the neighbors too. With the phones still out, no one knows much of anything."

"Ok," Dr. Burke said. "I suppose it's all right."

"Thanks, Dad," Amy said, pushing the old red Spirit Flyer out the front door onto the walk. Her father followed her outside.

"You can go ride your bike for a few hours, but if anything strange starts to happen, come home immediately," he warned.

"Strange like what?"

"Well, if you see anyone with guns of any kind, just get away fast," he said. "There have been reports of roving gangs with guns. They've been looting stores and robbing people. We haven't had that trouble around here, but they're out there. Who knows what else could happen?"

Amy nodded. She certainly didn't want to see any gangs. She pedaled the old bicycle down the driveway and headed toward town. The place seemed so much quieter than usual. All the stores were closed. Some people stood in their yards and talked to their neighbors. A few cars prowled up and down the streets. And here and there, Amy saw children playing. But she had only one thing on her mind. She pedaled north up Oak Street and then turned west on Cemetery Road. The big balloon tires rolled easily down the pavement of the old road.

From the distance, Amy could see that the walls around Bicycle Hills were down. She pedaled faster, past the locked gates of the Goliath factory and past the cemetery. She coasted to a stop when she got closer to what was left of Bicycle Hills. The field looked as if a big bomb had hit it. All that seemed to be left was a great hole. The hills were gone, everything was gone and all that was left was a giant blackened pit, as if even the dirt had been burned. The large hole went almost all the way to the road. There were two warning signs blinking on and off where the hole came closest to the pavement. Amy knew that in normal conditions, the highway department would have put up a barricade or something right away. But things hadn't been normal in Centerville these last few days. Amy looked at the hole and wondered if things would ever be normal again.

"Amy!" a voice yelled. Amy whirled around. Three old red bicycles were softly gliding down through the air about twenty feet away. John Kramar was in front, a huge smile on his face. The old bikes touched down and rolled to a stop. Susan Kramar and Daniel Bayley seemed just as happy as John to see her.

"You got a Spirit Flyer too," Susan said. "That's great. Other kids got them as well. There are at least twenty-five of us now, if not more. We'll have a great group."

"It just showed up in my room the morning after Halloween," Amy said with a smile.

"That was some night," Daniel Bayley said seriously. "I didn't think it would ever end."

"I thought it was going to be the end," John said.

The other children nodded silently. They stared at the pit that had been Bicycle Hills.

"To think we could be down under all that if it wasn't for you," Amy said.

"We didn't do much," John said. "It was the kings and the Aggeloi."

"A lot of people didn't come out as well," Susan Kramar said softly. "Since my dad is the sheriff, he gets reports. All sorts of weird and strange things happened that Halloween night. Those two older kids that weren't released from the arms of the Daimones are missing. Her name was Mary and his name was Brent, my dad said. Lots of kids in other towns are missing too."

"But that's hardly news considering what's going on in the rest of the world," Daniel Bayley added. "It's like Goliath planned it that way, so everyone would be confused. Who cares about missing kids when they have to worry about nuclear warheads and satellite weapons. My mother has been really scared. She went to her office the other day at the factory, and they told her all about it. She won't even tell my sister and me what she knows, except that there was a war. I think they also threatened to fire her. In fact, she may already be fired, for all I know."

"My dad won't say much either," Susan said. "He said there are still too many rumors and there's no point in scaring us if they don't have to. No one really seems to know for sure yet what all the damages were."

"My dad said the satellite defense systems worked and knocked out a lot of missiles," Amy replied. "But there were submarines that launched missiles from the sea and some of those got through on the coastlines."

"That's why the government is all in a shambles and the military is in control," Daniel said. "When there is a state of emergency and martial law, they can do almost anything. My mom said everything will be different for a while. Maybe it will never go back the way it was before."

"In a lot of places, private police are in control," John Kramar said. "In the cities, there have been a lot of gangs breaking into stores and stuff, just like terrorists. People in the ORDER party have organized and are working alone or in some places with the military police to stop the gangs. A lot of people in Centerville want to do the same thing."

"But there aren't any gangs here, are there?" Amy asked. She remembered her father's warning.

"No one has reported anything like that to my dad," Susan said. "But a lot of the townspeople don't want to take any chances, so they want to get a bigger police force."

"You mean your dad might not be sheriff anymore?" Amy asked.

"Well, he might not have been anyway, since he was up for re-election," Susan said simply. "He wasn't in the ORDER party, and now they have a lot of power and support. But since the elections have been called off, no one knows for sure who will be in control."

"But he's in control so far," John added quickly, a note of pride in his voice. "A lot of people still support him."

"I wonder if school will start up again?" Amy asked.

"It's funded through the government," Daniel said. "And since there's so much confusion on so many levels of government and banking systems, I bet school won't open for at least two weeks, maybe longer. Maybe school will never open."

"There has to be school," John Kramar said. "Doesn't there?"

"Who knows?" Daniel replied.

"It's scary, I think," Amy said.

"It doesn't look good," Susan agreed. "No one ever really thought things would go so far. That's what I hear people saying."

"The whole country is messed up, that's for sure," John said grimly.

"The whole world has gone crazy," Daniel added. "Our country could have gotten hit a lot worse. I heard someone say that crazy General Ragamoon in Northern Africa, the terrorist with his own bombs, caused his whole country to be wiped out. Everyone bombed them."

The children were silent. On Halloween night, none of them had heard any bombs. All they had heard was deadly quiet.

"I wonder what will happen?" Amy said.

"No one knows for sure but the kings," John said. "But you can read what they say in *The Book of the Kings*. Before the Prince of Kings returns to rule and set up his kingdom forever, things are supposed to get really bad on earth. I've heard some people say they think this is the time before his return."

"I'd like to borrow that book," Amy said.

"Sure," John said with a smile.

The children all looked down silently in the deadened pit that was once Bicycle Hills.

"My dad said that Sloan Favor is real sick," Amy said. "Ever since Halloween night he's been in bed with a high fever."

"I've heard of other kids being sick," Susan said. "My mom mentioned it. No one would believe it could have been caused from stuff happening out here, though. When you talk about the Deeper World, a lot of people just laugh at you."

"No one was laughing that night," Amy said, remembering the great cobra and the Daimones. "I wonder if the other children missing that night in other towns were taken by the Daimones?"

"I bet they were," John said. "On Halloween night, they seemed to have extra power or something."

"But why wouldn't the Aggeloi save all the kids everywhere?" Amy asked. "Why were those two other kids taken, yet Sloan got free?"

"I don't know," John Kramar said. "I've been wondering the same things. I don't understand why they do one thing and not others."

"I think some people just make bad choices and get in trouble before they realize they're dealing with forces from the Deeper World," Susan said. "In *The Book of the Kings* it says people are swayed by the pull of their chains and that all kinds of bad things can happen."

"Well, everyone got a good view of the Deeper World on Halloween," John Kramar said. "They got to see the Domain of Darkness and the Kingdom of the Three Kings both."

Amy nodded her head up and down, remembering. "I don't think anyone can forget it when they see the Prince of Kings," Amy said. "I know I couldn't. You can run away to avoid looking at his gaze again, I guess, but deep down, you can never forget."

"No one looks right inside you like him, that's for sure," John said.

The children were quiet for a few minutes.

"Well, it's no time to be morbid," Daniel Bayley said, breaking the silence. "We have work to do. Amy is right. A lot of kids did see the kingdom that night, and we need to tell them about the kings and how they can get rid of their chains. People don't have to be slaves, controlled by the chain. And until the Kingson returns, we're the ones to show them ways into the kingdom."

"I'd like to know more about this bike," Amy said. "Will my bike fly too?" As soon as the words were out of her mouth, the old red bike began to move. Amy yelped in surprise. The other children smiled immediately. "I'm not pedaling!" Amy yelled.

"That's ok," John Kramar said as he pedaled up beside her. "Just hang on."

Without a sound, the front tire on Amy's old red bicycle left the pavement, followed by the rear tire. Soon she was ten feet off the ground

and picking up speed. She felt a burst of fear, but then she was calm. The other children were right beside her in the air, smiles on their faces, the wind blowing their hair.

"Where are we going?" Amy asked loudly.

"Wherever the kings want," John yelled.

"There!" Daniel Bayley pointed ahead. Up ahead in the air, the clouds seemed to be opening up the sky to a beautiful place. Lots of the old red bikes with riders were flying toward it from all different directions.

"Just wait till we play flight tag!" John Kramar yelled out in glee. The beautiful place opened up even wider to receive the riders.

"The kingdom," Amy said to herself. Looking into the kingdom, she knew she was at home at last, a home that would never be blown away by bombs or destroyed by war or death. The sky peeled back farther and farther in a rush of wind. Suddenly she knew deep inside that no matter what the future held, there would always be the kingdom. And if the kingdom were near, she would never be far from the presence of the kings themselves.